HI, THIS IS CONCHITA

AND OTHER STORIES

HI, THIS IS CONCHITA

AND OTHER STORIES

Santiago Roncagliolo

Translated by Edith Grossman

Two Lines Press

Hola, Pussy al habla y otros cuentos © 2013 by Santiago Roncagliolo
Translation © 2013 by Edith Grossman
All rights reserved.

Published by Two Lines Press
582 Market Street, Suite 700, San Francisco, CA 94104
www.twolinespress.com

"Butterflies Fastened with Pins" first published in *The Coffin Factory*.

ISBN 978-1-931883-22-1

Library of Congress Control Number: 2012949293

Design by Ragina Johnson
Cover design by Gabriele Wilson
Cover Photo by Philip Habib/Gallery Stock

Printed in the United States of America

This project is supported in part by an award from the National Endowment for the
Arts and a grant from Amazon.com.

Contents

Hi, This Is Conchita

1

Despoiler

135

Butterflies Fastened with Pins

155

The Passenger Beside You

169

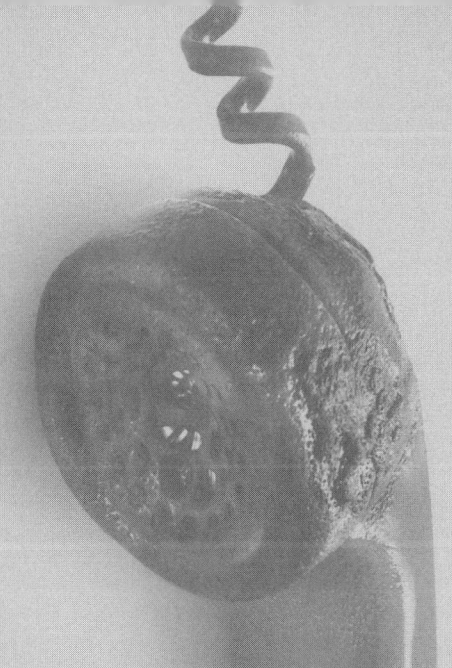

HI, THIS IS CONCHITA

(415) 952–3144

12:14 AM

— Hi. This is Conchita.

— Hi, Conchita.

— Mmmhh…You have a real man's voice.

— You think so?

— Oh, yeah. It makes me hot just to hear you.

— That's good. I'm hot too.

— Really? My voice gets you hot? Very hot?

— Yeah, you have a…very sensual voice, oh yeah.

— What do you like best?

— Well…I don't know. Since I can't see you and all, I don't…

— I have long blond hair, curly and down to my tits… mmhhh…I like to play with my curls and my nipples…

— What are they like? Your nipples, I mean…

— Pink and big.

— Ohhh…Like two pink pacifiers?

— Yeah, exactly like that…Are you sucking them for me now?

— Yeah…

— I like how you do it. Suck them, suck them like that…

— Yeah…

— Where are you?

— Now?

— Yeah, now.

— In my…office, you might say.

— Do you have a desk?

— I have a desk and a coffee machine.

— You have me lying face down on your desk. Do you want to know what my ass is like?

— What's it like?

— It's round and very soft, you can open it with your fingers and stick them between my cheeks.

— Like this?

— Ahhh…yeah, like that…

— What am I doing now?

— You're sitting in the chair and spreading my cheeks with your fingers…You stick one in, then another, while I twist around it's so delicious…

— I like that, yeah…

— I'm so hot and my tits are slapping against the top of the desk. Can you hear it, like clapping?

— Yeah, yeah, yeah…Where's my cock?

— Mmmhh…I haven't taken it out yet, but now I can't stand it anymore and I lower my hand and begin to rub it through your trousers…

— Take it out for me, please, take it out.

— Do you want me to take it out?

— Oh yeah!

— Say it louder…

— Take it out, mmmhh, take it out!…

— That's it, now I turn around. I'm still on the desk, on all fours, but now my mouth is near your fly, I begin to bite it on top. Do you like it?

— I love it.

— Now I move forward. So I won't fall, I lean on the coffee machine. I get burned…

— You can't.

— What?

— You can't lean on the coffee machine. It's on the other… on the other side of the room. The desk is in front of the window and the coffee machine's beside the door. Maybe you can lean, let me see, on a file cabinet.

— On a what?

— A file cabinet. It's like a closet, but for files.

— A file cabinet then.

— Use this one, the green one.

— OK, the green one.

— Then you didn't get burned.

— I did get burned, but by your body.

— My body.

— Your body, yeah, so I'm opening your fly with my hands and lift up your underwear with my teeth, ooh, yeah…It's stiff, it's so hard, so big…

— Do you want to suck it?

— My hand's in your underwear now because I'm caressing your balls. Do you like it?

— Yeah, I love it, I hadn't noticed. Sorry.

— Do you want me to take off your trousers?

— Yeah.

— You've raised yourself up a little from the chair and now I'm taking your trousers down your legs, caressing and biting your thighs.

— What am I doing?

— You're looking at me. I'm hair-free, not a single hair on my twat, like a baby.

— Oh.

— I'm wet, my juices have smeared the whole desk…

— Ahhh…

— And my sweat…

— And your sweat…

— Do you like it?

— Yeah, yeah…

— Do you want to lick it?

— Ufff…

— Lick me from my neck to my belly button…

— And your twat?

— No, not my twat, because now I'm sitting on you, oh, yeah, you've nailed me, filled me right up, you move it around…

— …I move it around…

— You burn me.

— Yeah.

— And it goes in and out, in and out, like that, more, more, more, ooohhh…

— Aaaahhh…

— …A little more…

— Mooo-ooo-ooore…

— …

— Go on, go on!

— …Now I'm getting back on the desk, you're going to stand, and stick it to me from behind. OK?

— Yeeeeaaah…

— Give it to me, give it to me, ufff, mmmhhmm…

— You like it?

— Ohhh, yeah, yeah…

— Brilliant, Conchita.

— Ohhh…What did you say?

— I said that's brilliant, Conchita.

— Brilliant.

— Yeah, brilliant.

— Are you doing it?

— What?

— What do you mean what? What are we talking about?

— About whether I'm sticking it in you?

— Well, yeah. Are you doing it?

— Yeah.

— OK.

— …

— …

— …It's just that…

— Yeah?

— No, nothing…

— Everything OK? You want me to suck it a little more?

— …No, no. I'm all through.

— Already?

— Yeah, already.

— Ah.

— Did it seem too fast?

— No, it was fine. You're the best.

— Really?

— Oh, sure. It was incredible, mmmhhh…

— You liked it?

— You think I didn't?

— No, it's not that.

— What, then?

— Nothing.

— OK.

— OK.

— Fine.

— Yeah, fine.

— …

— Well, thanks, Conchita.

— Will you call me again?

— Yeah.

— Promise?

— Sure.

— Then it's fine.

— Bye, Conchita.

— Bye-bye.

(415) 937–0353

9:33 AM

— Welcome to customer service. If you need information regarding any of our products, press 1. To find out about bills and fees, press 2. If you want to know how to receive more packaged services, press 3. If...

2

— One moment please. We're here to serve you better. Taaaa-ta-ta-taaa-ta-ta-ta-ta-ra-ra-raaaa-tiiiii-ti-ti-tiiii-taa-ra-ra-ra-ra-ta-ra-ra-taaaa-ta-ta-taraaaa-tu-ri-ru taaaa-ta-ta-taaaa-ta-ta-ta-ta-ra-ra-raaaa-tiiiii-ti-ti-tiiii-taa-ra-ra-ra-ra-ta-ra-ra-taaaa-ta-ta-ta-raaaatu-ri-ru-taaaa-ta-ta-taaaa-ta-ta-ta-ta-ra-ra-raaaa-tiiiii-ti-ti-tiii-taa-ra-ra-ra-ra-ta-ra-ra-taaaa-ta-ta-ta-raaaa-tu-ri-ri-taaaa-ta-ta-taaaa-ta-ta-ta-ta-ra-ra-raaaa-tiiiii-ti-ti-tiiii-taa-ra-ra-ra-ra-ta-ra-ra-taaaa-ta-ta-ta-raaaa-tu-ri-ru-taaaa-ta-ta-ta-aaa-ta-ta-ta-ta-ra-ra-raaaa-tiiiii-ti-ti-tiiii-taa-ra-ra-ra-ra-ra-ta-ra-ra-taaaa-ta-ta-ta-raaaa-tu-ri-ru- This is Lola. How may I help you?
— Hello?
— Yes, good morning?

— How are you? I'm calling because you've sent me the same bill twice and I'd like…

— Your name please?

— Godínez…my last name's Godínez…The fact is you've charged me twice…

— Your ID number?

— X-3459362-Y. I had the bill linked to my bank, so you've withdrawn the sum from my account…

— Godínes with an S or Godínez with a Z?

— With a Z. I like to know how I can recup…

— I'll transfer you to a sales representative.

— Hello? Hello?

— One moment, please. We're here to serve you better. Taaaa-ta-ta-taaaa-ta-ta-ta-ta-ra-ra-raaaa-tiiiii-ti-ti-tiiii-taa-ra-ra-ra-ra-ra-ta-ra-ra-taaaa-ta-ta-ta-raaaa-tu-ri-ru-taaaa-ta-ta-taaaa-ta-ta-ta-ta-ra-ra-raaaa-tiiiii-ti-ti-tiiii-taa-ra-ra-ra-ra-ra-ta-ra-ra-taaaa-ta-ta-ta-raaaa-ru-ri-ru-taaaa-ta-ta-taaaa-ta-ta-ta-ta-ra-ra-raaaa-tiiiii-ti-ti-tiiii-taa-ra-ra-ra-ra-ra-ta-ra-ra-taaaa-ta-ta-ta-raaaa-tu-ri-ru-taaaa-ta-ta-ta-ta-ra-ra-raaaa-tiiiii-ti-ti-tiiii-taa-ra-ra-ra-ra-ta-ra-ra-taaaa-ta-ta-ta-raaaaa-tu-ri-ru-taaa-ta-ta-ta-taaaa-ta-ta-ta-ta-ra-ra-raaaa-tiiiii-ti-ti-tiiii-taa-ra-ra-ra-ra-ra-ta-ra-ra-taaaa-ta-ta-ta-raaaa-tu-ri-ru- This is Jorge. How may I help you?

— Well, you see, you've charged me twi…

— Your name, please?

— I already gave my name to Lola.

— Who?

— Lola.

— …

— The girl who was on before.

— I'd love to know the details, but this is a customer service center. Are you a customer who needs service?

— Yes, you charged me twice in the same month…

— Your name, please.

— Godínez. My last name is Godínez.

— Your ID number?

— X-3459362-Y

— 9363?

— 62. 9362.

— Aha. Go ahead, Señor Godínez.

— You've charged twice in the same month and…

— Twice?

— Twice. At the same time.

— Twice at the same time. Aha. You should pay, and after processing your complaint, we'll reimburse you on the next bill.

— But I already paid. You withdrew it from my account.

— Let me see…Can you wait a second?

— Please, don't put on the music.

— What music?

— The music that plays while I'm waiting.

— But I have to put on music.

— But I don't want it. I'd be grateful if…

— If we don't put on the music, how will you wait?

— I already waited.

— Aha.

— And I don't have time now, you know? I'm at work and…

— You don't have time now?

— No, I really don't.

— I understand, sir. Thank you very much for your query and remember: we're here to serve you better.

Click.

— Hello? Jorge? Are you there? Hello?

(415) 952–3148

2:47 PM

— Yes?

— Don?

— M…Mary?

— Are you disappointed to hear my voice?

— No, of course not. It's just—I'm surprised, that's all.

— Really? Well, I was surprised not to hear yours…

— Mary…

— …Not to hear it last night, or Monday, or Sunday, when you said you'd call.

— Listen, it's not a good time to talk…

— "It's not a good time to talk, it's not a good time to talk." And when is it a good time, if you don't mind my asking?

— Is it all right if I call you this evening after we close the deal?

— Deal? What the devil are you…

— Yes, it's just that right now…I'm speaking with another

client…

— You don't have…

— Then I'll call you, all right?

— You're not there with a girlfriend, are you, Don? I mean…

— No, no complication…

— I mean you deceive your wife with me. And you're deceiving me with another woman, aren't you?

— You know our motto is keeping faith with our clients.

— Don, stop talking like a bank commercial! Why haven't you called me in three days? Do you think you can play with me? Do you? You think I'm your weekend toy, don't you? Your tramp!

— Well look, I'll find that…that information right now, since it's urgent…

— Are you going to hang up on me?

— No, no, no, not at all. Right now I'm excusing myself for a few seconds, hold on, I'm walking down the hall to the bathroom…

— You don't have to describe the whole building to me, Don.

— And now that I'm in the bathroom and, yes it's empty, and…have you lost your mind?! Are you hysterical?!

— Ah, yes, now the real Don is back. And he's insulting me. He disappears the entire weekend and now he comes and…

— Mary, please…

— …insults me. Is that what you think? That I'm hysterical?

— Mary, don't…

— Because if you believe that you can take your roses and your invitations to fancy dinners and shove them up your ass. Do you hear?

— …Darling…

— Up your ass!

— You don't have to be like that…

— And how do I have to be, please? Tell me! How do I have to be?

— I had a hard weekend. Understand? My wife wanted to go out with the children, I couldn't get out of it…

— You had a hard weekend? And what about me, Don? Answer me! Didn't I have a difficult weekend, stuck in the apartment alone, waiting for you, you bastard?

— Mary, I have a client outside…

— So what?! Now you prefer your work to me? You treat me as if I were your wife. Ah, no, right. I not only matter to you less than your work, I matter less than your wife, you just…

— …Don't cry…

— …you just said…

— Mary, somebody's coming into the bathroom…

— …You want to hang up on me, fine. Hang up, if you want. But if you do, don't ever call me again, ever!

— Listen, have you spoken to the manager?

— What did you say?

— …I'm not talking to you…hold on…a kid just came into the bathroom…have you spoken to the manager? He's looking for you and seems to be in a very bad mood. That's right, go find him fast, kid…

— Of course it's a lie, you always lie. It's a lie, kid, don't believe him!

— Mary, can you be quiet? Do you want me to talk to you or not?

— Oh, Don…

— Oh, Mary…

— You've lost respect for me, you shut me up, you insult me, you don't call me…

— It isn't that, you know I love you, it's just a…complicated time. Understand?

— I guess I have no choice but to understand…

— Don't say that, Mary. Listen. I can invent a work conference this weekend. We could go to the country for a few days. Would you like that? You'd like it, wouldn't you?

— I don't know.

— Of course you would, I know how much you like the country…

— And if your wife wants you to stay?

— She won't, we just spent a weekend together and she must be sick of me.

— And we'll go riding?

— Of course. And I'll give you a bouquet of yellow roses, the kind you like.

— You don't have to bother.

— I will.

— Really?

— Oh, Mary, you know I can't lie to you.

— Am I still your little cream cake?

— You'll be that forever, darling.

— Say it.

— You're my little cream cake.

— Oh, Don.

— Oh, Mary.

— Oh, Don.

— All right, pumpkin, listen, I left my client alone and…

— Do you want me to hang up?

— No, of course I don't. I'll call you this evening, OK? I promise.

— You want me to hang up.

— Mary, I already explained to you…

— Well, I didn't understand.

— What is it? Why are you acting like this?

— I just don't know, Don. You always have so many things to do, and your family and your life and your success. I don't have anything, understand? Nothing but you.

— The only thing that matters to me is you…

— That's not true. If it were true, you'd get a divorce.

— Mary, we've already talked about this…

— You never want to talk about it, Don, and you always say we've talked about it.

— I'm going to get a divorce, Mary. My marriage doesn't work anymore. But I can't leave her now because of the kids, you know? They need a family.

— Your youngest son is twenty-three, Don.

— But even so it isn't easy. Even so, you can be sure I'll get a divorce, I'll get it… I'll get it before the end of the year…

— It's four years you've been saying that. I don't know how much longer I can put up with it.

— Mary, listen to me. You just have to have a little more patience, OK?

— No.

— What do you mean, no?

— Just no.

— What does that mean, Mary? You're not…

— I won't put up with it anymore.

— Mary…

— Either you tell your wife what's going on, or I will, Don.

— Wha…?

— You heard me.

— And if we talk this weekend in the country…

— There won't be any country or any weekend until you've told her…

— Right.

— If you don't, I will…

— I understand.

— I'm serious, Don! Don't you think I can do it?

— Of course you can, of course you can. You're absolutely right.

— Ah, I am?

— Give me this weekend, OK? Just this weekend. I'll tell her on Friday.

— On Friday, Don.

— Friday, right.

— And you'll move in with me on Saturday?

— Yeah, sure I will.

— Oh, Don…

— …

— We'll be very happy, won't we?

— We will, Mary. You can be sure of that.

— I love you.

— I love you.

— Here's an enormous kiss.

— Bye.

— …Don.

— Yeah?

— Friday.

— Friday. Sure. Bye.

(415) 496–6642

2:12 AM

— Hello, this is Esmeralda…

— Esmeralda, it's me. Listen to me, don't hang up…

— …I can't answer the phone right now, but leave your message and your number after the tone, and I'll get back to you as soon as I can. Ciao.

— Shit. Esmeralda, I know you're there. Please, pick up. Please…Shit.

(415) 952–3144

12:58 AM

— Hello?

— Conchita?

— Yeah.

— It's me.

— …

— Do you remember me?

— Ye…Yeah, sure. Mmmhh, how could I forget you…

— Good. The last time we talked, you know, you were a little…cold with me.

— I was?

— Maybe it was my fault…I don't know.

— I just wanted more from you, ooohhh, you get me so…

— Right. I hope…I didn't disappoint you or anything like that…

— Oh, no, it's just that I can't get enough of you…

— I think sometimes…I think I've disappointed women, you know?

— Why, when you're so…

— I don't know…

— So strong and so virile…

— I don't mean I couldn't…you know…

— Of course not…

— I always could, you know?

— …Mmmmhh…

— It's just that I…it's like they…

— Sure.

— Like I couldn't satisfy them or something…

— Unbelievable, yeah.

— But you're different, right?

— I'm yours.

— Yeah.

— What do you want to do today?

— I don't know…maybe…maybe something rough would be good…

— Where are you?

— In my office. I always call from here. It's…cheaper…

— You're a rascal…

— Ha, ha…yeah, I guess I am…

— Would you like a little pain?

— Well, I don't want you to think I'm…

— It's fine…

— Brilliant.

— Do you like me dressed in leather?

— Leather? Oooohh, yeah.

— Black leather, with a spiked collar…

— Yeah…

— Like your dog, I'm your dog…

— And me?

— And you? You're garbage. Is that all right?

— Perfect.

— You're just a piece of rotten meat.

— That's it, yeah. Do you have a…

— I have a whip with seven lashes, tipped in metal…

— Wow.

— …And I come in slamming the door of your office.

— Don't slam it too hard. It's just…the coffee machine's behind the door and…

— I don't care!

— Oh.

— I don't care about anything you say because you're a piece of shit. You hear me?

— That's it, more…

— You're a piece of shit that only deserves to lick the soles of my boots!

— You're wearing boots?

— They're high, they reach above my knee, and the heels are very high so…

— That's good…

— …So I can drive them into your face…

— Ow!

— Now I drag you down to the floor…

— Watch it! The file cabinet's rickety…

— Fuck your file cabinet! You hit your head on it, but I keep dragging you across the floor…

— …Oh, Conchita…

— Now I want you to lick my soles…

— Please, no…

— Lick them, you piece of shit!

— That's good…

— And you better leave them clean.

— Yes, Conchita.

— You like it?

— …it hurts…

— Take that, you shit!

— Ah!

— And take this! And this!

— That's enough, please…

— That's it, beg me…

— Please, please, please…

— Now I'm going to sit on your face and pull down your trousers…

— …Wait…

— Shut up! You're going to lick me, got it? And if you don't do it right, I'll whip you on your cock.

— …Yes, Conchita…

— Are you doing it?

— …It's just that…

— It's just what, you bastard?

— …I don't know if you've taken off your leather pants…

— Through the slit, imbecile! Don't you see it?

— Ahh, yeah, the slit…

— Take this for being an imbecile!

— Ouch!

— Are you doing it?

— Mmfff, bbrrfff, scchmk…

— Take that!

— Aaahhh! But I was licking…

— Shut up! Turn around.

— But what…

— I didn't tell you to ask questions! Turn around.

— Yeah, like this, is this all right?

— Raise your ass, I want to see you crawl…

— I'm crawling, I'm under the desk…

— Now don't move!

— What are you going to do, Conchita? I think…

— You don't think anything, faggot!

— Right…What's this? Balls?

— Yeah, balls…

— You're not going…

— If you stiffen up, it'll hurt more…

— It's just, Conchita, I think we're passing…Aaah!

— Did you like that? Of course you liked it, that's what you want, sissy!

— No more, please…

— I want to hear you beg!

— Aaaaahhhh! Enough! Enough!

— Say you like it.

— I love it…

— Say it loud!

— I love it!

— Without crying, you piece of shit!

— I love it! Aaaaah! Yessss! I really like it!

— You're a disgusting piece of shit.

— Yes, I am…it's true…

— Don't tell me I'm right, take that!

— Aaaahhh! I'm not, I'm not!...

— Did you call me a liar?

— Ouch! Aaaaah!

— Want more? Ah?

— ...

— I said do you want more!

— ...

— Are you there? Can you hear me? Is everything all right?

— Oh, yeah, Conchita...it's just that...

— Oh, handsome, did I hit you too hard?

— A little, yeah...the truth is...

— You want me...

— It hurts here, see?

— I see, darling, I'm sorry, I didn't want to cross...

— It's fine, don't worry...I hope...

— Do you want me to caress you?

— Yes, please...

— Here?

— There.

— That's it...that's it...it's over, everything's fine now...

— Conchita?

— Sssshhh, tell me...

— You're the best, Conchita...you...

— No, you're the best, you're a tiger...

— Do you really think so?

— Sure I do.

— Thanks, Conchita...

— Will you call me again?

— Sure I will. I feel there's something between us...something special, right?

— Yeah, very special…

— Thanks, Conchita…

— Sure you don't want me to caress you some more?

— It's fine…You…must have things to do and…

— No, it's fine…

— Don't worry about me.

— All right, whatever you want…

— Conchita…

— Yeah?

— …

— Yeah?

— …Thank you.

— Right.

— Bye, Conchita.

— Bye-bye.

(415) 937–0353

10:06 AM

— Welcome to our customer service center. If you need information about any of our products, press 1. For information regarding bills and rates, press 2. If you…

2

— One moment please. We're here to serve you better. Taaaa-ta-ta-taaa-ta-ta-ta-ta-ra-ra-raaa-tiiiii-ti-ti-tiii-taa-ra-ra-ra-ra-ra-ta-ra-ra-taaa-ta-ta-ta-raaaa-tu-ri-ru-taaaa-ta-ta-taaaa-ta-ta-ta-ta-ra-ra-raaaa-tiiiii-ti-ti-tiiiitaa-ra-ra-ra-ra-ra-ta-ra-ra-taaaa-ta-ta-ta-raaaa-tu-ri-tu-taaaa-ta-ta-taaaa-ta-ta-ta-ta-ra-ra-raaaa-tiiiii-ti-ti-tiiii-taa-ra-ra-ra-ra-ra-ra-ta-ra-taaaa-ta-ta-ta-raaaa-tu-ri-ru-taaaa-ta-ta-ta-aaa-ta-ta-ta-ta-ra-ra-raaaa-tiiiii-ti-ti-tiiii-taaa-ra-ra-ra-ra-ra-ta-ra-ra-taaaa-ta-ta-ta-raaaa-tu-ri-ru-taaaa-ta-ta-taaaa-ta-ta-ta-ta-ra-ra-raaaa-tiiiii-ti-ti-tiiiitaa-ra-ra-ra-ra-ra-ta-ra-ra-taaaa-ta-ta-ta-raaatu-ri-ru- This is Trini, how may I help you?

— I'd like to speak with the sales representative Jorge, please.

— One moment, please. We're here to serve you better. Taaaa-ta-ta-taaaa-ta-ta-ta-ta-ra-ra-raaaa-tiiiii-ti-ti-tiiii-taa-ra-ra-ra-ra-ra-ta-ra-ra-taaa-ta-ta-ta-raaaa-tu-ri-ru-ta-aaa-ta-ta-taaaa-ta-ta-ta-ta-ra-ra-raaaa-tiiiii-ti-ti-tiii-taa-ra-ra-ra-ra-ra-ta-ra-ra-taaa-ta-ta-ta-raaaa-tu-ri-ru-taaaa-ta-ta-ta-ra-ra-raaaa-tiiiii-ti-ti-tiiii-taa-ra-ra-ra-ra-ra-ta-ra-ra-taaaa-ta-ta-ta-raaaa-tu-ri-ru-taaaa-ta-ta-taaaa-ta-ta-ta-ra-ra-raaaa-tiiiii-ti-ti-tiiii-taa-ra-ra-ra-ra-ra-ta-ra-ra-taaaa-ta-ta-ta-raaaa-tu-ri-ru-taaaa-ta-ta-taaaa-ta-ta-ta-ta-ra-ra-raaaa-tiiiii-ti-ti-tiiii-taa-ra-ra-ra-ra-ra-ta-ra-ra-taaaa-ta-ta-ta-raaaa-tu-ri-ru- This is Jorge. How may I help you?

— This is Godínez.

— …

— Godínez, with a Z.

— Yes?

— I'm calling because…you see…you've charged me twice for the same bill and…

— Your ID number, please?

— I called yesterday…I don't know whether…

— Excuse me? Your ID number is…

— X-3459362-Y

— 63?

— 62. 9362.

— Señor Godínez?

— Yes.

— How may I help you, Señor Godínez?

— Well, you see—you've charged me twice for the same bill and…

— For May?

— April. And I've lost the money because you…

— I'm sorry. We're dealing only with May bills.

— But that money…

— You should have called in May.

— Right, but I only noticed it a week ago and…

— But now we're dealing only with May, Señor Godínez.

— Only May.

— Just May.

— And is there someplace where I could…

— You could send the original and a copy of your bills to Palomares 5, Suite 6C, along with a written complaint and a certificate of ownership of the property…

— Property?

— Yes, property. It's to be certain…

— It's just that I'm not the…

— To be certain you're really who…

— I'm not the owner…I rent…

— The owner of the property has to take care of the transaction.

— Right. But the owner lives in Sudan.

— In Sudan.

— In Sudan, yes. He's lived there for…

— I'm sorry, Señor Godínez.

— There must be some way to…

— You can bring a notarized letter from the owner saying that in fact you live there, certified by a Sudanese notary, authenticated at the embassy, and translated by a certified translator into…

— There's no Sudanese embassy here.

— Are you sure?

— I checked, yes…You see, I make a deposit to his account every month and…

— I'm sorry, Señor Godínez.

— But it's…

— Is there something else I can help you with?

— Something else?

— You're a customer, and this is our customer service center. Do you need service?

— Well, no…I think that…no.

— Thank you very much for your query and remember: we're here to serve you better.

— Right.

(415) 938–7716

11:30 P.M

— Yes?

— Hello?

— Yes?

— Are you Reginaldo?

— Maybe.

— Hello, my name is Don. Um…

— Yes?

— Do you need my last name?

— No.

— A friend gave me your number for a…matter that needs to be settled.

— Right.

— …

— And so?

— And so what, Reginaldo?

— Exactly. And so what, Don?

— Will you make an appointment with me?

— No.

— Are we going to arrange things by phone?

— What do you want us to do? Have a party?

— No, but…I don't know, it doesn't seem the kind of thing you can do by phone.

— What thing?

— That's exactly what I can't say on the phone.

— All right, for starters tell me who we're talking about.

— Her name's Mary…she's…a friend.

— A friend.

— Well, not such a friend, of course, or I wouldn't be…well.

— Well.

— She's very nice, I don't want you to think that…

— It doesn't matter what I think.

— No of course not, but in any event…

— It doesn't matter.

— Right.

— I'll need more information about her.

— She's young. Yeah. She's young and has curly blond hair that comes down to her breasts, and thick, pink nipples, like two pacifiers…

— I was referring to her address or something like that.

— Palomares 5, Sixth floor, A.

— P-A-L…

— Palomares, yeah.

— O-M-A…

— With S at the end.

— I heard you.

— When? When will you do it?

— That depends. Do you just want to shake her up or do we blow her away?

— What?

— Because I can just give her a scare, you know, you put a weapon in her mouth and say 'Listen, bitch, if I see you cheating on him again…' What's your name?

— Don.

— 'If you cheat on Don again, I'll put a bullet in your brain, blah, blah, blah.' Generally it works.

— Blah, blah, blah.

— That's it.

— I don't think it'll work in this case, you see, she isn't cheating on me.

— And how do you know that?

— Well, I don't know, but…

— You trust her.

— No, it's just that…

— You don't trust her? Then we'll give her a scare.

— I'd prefer the other thing…

— We blow her away.

— I wouldn't call it that, it's just that, basically I love her…

— Right. And she has an insurance policy you love too. Right?

— No…she isn't my wife.

— Then maybe the money won't go to you. Have you thought about that?

— It isn't for money.

— Right.

— In fact, she doesn't have a cent.

— I understand.

— I picked her up at a bar where she sang at night. She

lived…she lived in a trailer and like that…

— And you took her in.

— Yeah, you could say that.

— You're generous, you know?

— Thanks.

— Normally I don't shoot on orders from people so…

— I'd be grateful if you avoided words like that. It's just that by phone…

— It's better.

— Yeah?

— This way you don't see my face, and I don't see yours. It's practical.

— Sure.

— So, you took her in.

— Yeah.

— And then?

— And then we became closer and closer, you know? She… understood me…I mean she understands me…she isn't… well, not yet…I mean…

— She understands you more than your wife.

— A lot more. My wife and I…it's like we speak different languages, you know?

— Yeah.

— I mean, it's not that things are going badly but…

— It's not like it was before.

— Exactly, it's not like it was before.

— And why don't…why don't you…

— Get a divorce?

— It's cheaper.

— No, I assure you it isn't, in my case. Besides, sure, Mary…
she's fine but…

— She isn't a wife…

— …You know everything that involves and…

— …And people and your property and your life and your
success…

— …Like I say…

— You'd rather she didn't suffer…

— That would be very good of you, it would be very…

— It's nothing.

— …Generous, on your part.

— Maybe you'd like to tell her something…I don't know…
in those final mom…

— Better not.

— It always helps to have a smile when…

— I'll invite her to dinner beforehand. I'll tell her…

— I don't know if that's enough…

— I'll tell her I've left my wife, that I love her, that I'll move
in with her that same night, things like that.

— That would be good.

— Yeah.

— In my heart, that's what I want. I mean…

— Sure.

— …I mean I'm not a monster or anything…

— No, of course not.

— I'd really like to move in with her and spend some time
together.

— Right.

— …She…She's very affectionate with me.

— Sure.

— Sometimes…sometimes we don't even…don't even have sex. You know? We just…

— Talk.

— We talk and she makes cream cakes and then we watch TV….It's what I like best…

— Your wife doesn't…

— She doesn't compare.

— Sure.

— It's a shame things have to be this way, don't you think so? In other circumstances maybe…

— Maybe, yeah.

— Well.

— I'll leave you a message with my account number for the advance…

— I was told you'd do it for ten thousand…

— In a case like this, fifteen.

— What do you mean a case like this? What's special about this case?

— She's a very good person.

— Right, that's true, but it's not worth five thousand…

— Thirteen.

— Twelve.

— Twelve and a half. Fair enough?

— OK.

— Bye, Don, thanks.

— Thank you. It's always good to talk to someone.

(415) 496–6642

2:12 A.M

— Hello, this is Esmeralda. I can't come to the phone right now, but leave your message and your number after the tone and I'll get back to you as soon as I can. Ciao.

— The adult channel is showing "I Came with the Wind," tonight, my darling Esmeralda. If you had cable, you could watch it. But since you don't have cable, or a boyfriend with cable, anymore, you can't. Don't worry, you're not missing much. The costumes are awful. Right now the big orgy between Scarlett O!, her black maid, her husband, her father, and her horse has just begun. It's the best part, yeah. In fact, the rest of the movie isn't worth much. I know because I've watched it seven times in the last fourteen days. The adult channel repeats movies a lot; we knew that, though, didn't we? Well, I've confirmed it in the two weeks since you left and my right hand has been my one remaining faithful companion. My right hand, eighteen pizza boxes, and one hundred twenty-two cans of beer. It amuses me to count them. In fact, recently I've been counting everything: cans, neon signs, the number of people who go to the movies next door, days, hours, nanoseconds, the times I think about you—which is certainly not many. Did you know that for the midnight show at the movie theater across the street, exactly twenty-two more people go into the movie house on Fridays than on Thursdays. That's exact, the same thing has happened for two weeks. Twenty-two more. And none of those twenty-two people is me, and none of them is you either. I thought you'd go to the movies by yourself occasionally, or maybe with a girlfriend, but you must have changed theaters, I guess you found one closer to your house, because you can't sleep here any more and it's dangerous to walk by yourself at night, right? Yeah. You never liked walking by yourself at night. Maybe that's why I'm assuming you found somebody to walk with you, not because he's going to do anything special if a mugger approaches or something, but just because you don't want to walk by yourself, that's all. He doesn't have to be handsome or especially strong or anything, just walk with you when you're no longer one of the average of sixty-two patrons at the bar in the Black & White at midnight, remain with you when you find yourself among the average of twenty-six people on the street at 1:30, the time you leave the bar, and stay beside you on the way home as the average number of heads shrinks until you reach the door of the elevator in your building, where there will be only two, and then cross the threshold of your apartment, where the usual population without me is one, and go into your room, sure, because you never liked sleeping by yourself either. After all, maybe walking can be done in small stretches of three hundred meters, but sleeping alone, no, because every night lasts the same amount of time and is equally dark, but the empty space in your bed has grown in recent weeks, and the average has to be regained. But I didn't call to bore you with numbers, Esmeralda, I really only wanted to tell you about the movie. The actor playing Clark Gable is sticking it in the mouth of one of the Confederate widows. It's to comfort her, I think, I didn't pay much attention to the dialogue. You did pay attention to that, I always thought movies should be silent, after all, who listens to what they're saying? But you did listen and could recall entire scenes, especially those romantic comedies with Meg Ryan that in the past two weeks I haven't had to watch, thank God. Because it's time you knew I detest Meg Ryan, Esmeralda, I hate everything about her: her spoiled little girl's eyes, her spoiled little girl's blond hair, her spoiled little girl's body with almost no tits. I think there's a plastic surgery clinic that specializes in spoiled little girls because they all look alike and all of them taken together don't have two kilos of chest. But don't make me ramble, the fact is that for me Meg Ryan is repulsive and detestable, and I agreed to watch the ninety-three minutes of "French Kiss" only because it was our first date and I wanted you to notice me, yeah, I wanted you to notice me, imagine, I even told you how much I liked that imbecile Meg Ryan and then I had to suffer through her next four pictures, which is exactly how long our relationship lasted, four of that moron's movies, but now I can tell you that I never liked her, I watched them thinking only that afterward we'd walk the less than three hundred meters to my house and spend the night in the increased population density of my bed, the first ten minutes talking about the movie and the rest of the night doing all the things Meg Ryan doesn't do but Scarlett O! does. Now, I'd take you to see "Carnal Olympics II," which is the worst of the sequels, because you don't matter to me and neither does Meg Ryan, and I don't even think about how there could be twenty-four people instead of twenty-two at the midnight show on the weekend. It doesn't even occur to me that the numerical difference could be us, sitting in the third row center because you always forget your glasses, though in fact I know you don't forget them but just hate to wear them because you don't want to be seen in glasses, and I know that's stupid because you look beautiful in glasses, damn, you look like a spoiled little girl with intellectual pretensions, adorable, especially when your bangs, like Meg Ryan's, fall over the frames, but at this point none of that is relevant because I simply don't care. I don't care about anything that has to do with you, not anything. I'm satisfied with my right hand, it's always been with me, through all of that idiot's movies and much longer than that, and it fulfills functions as important as yours, though it doesn't whisper pretty things from romantic comedies in my ear, and it doesn't wake me with coffee and bread that's burned from trying to toast it in the oven, but at least it'll never leave and if it does, it will have to be in a horrible accident from which I probably won't get out alive and you won't know about it because there won't be anyone to tell you about it because all our friends turned out to be your friends. Ah, that's another thing, you could give me back at least one of my friends, even if it's that bastard Miki who you put down so much. The cretin hasn't answered any of my calls, and I invited him to come over and watch the adult channel and have pizza and beer, a guys' night, but no. And I don't know whether to feel bad because that dummy doesn't answer my calls or because I really need to call that dummy and want him to answer. The last time I left a message on his answering machine it was everything you said about him, I didn't do it to fuck with you, Esmeralda, but just because it seemed to me he ought to know you thought he was a radish in trousers, that you said he was the proof God doesn't exist, because God wouldn't have been able to create anything as flawed as "that mental defective Miki." All those intellectual jokes you liked to tell when you wore your glasses and looked adorable, remember? I also told him you said his mother didn't give birth to him but shat him out—not a very intellectual joke, right? But actually, I was the one who said that but you laughed when I said it, so it wasn't much of a lie. Or Angela, at least, you could give Angela back, she was something of a snob but at least she refused to see Meg Ryan movies, which is more than we can say of you, and I'm sure she wanted to go to bed with me; you'll laugh, sure, but sometimes we'd be in the kitchen and I felt a certain magnetism, a certain animal attraction, like the kind between Scarlett O! and the horse, you know? In fact, Angela came by one day last week and pretended to be surprised when I told her you and I weren't together any-more, but I know it was a lie, she knew and had come to see me. I even took the pizza boxes and cans off the bed and invited her to watch the adult channel, but she didn't stay very long, not wanting to feel like she was betraying you so soon. It doesn't matter, I'll let some time pass and give her another chance, which she'll jump at because by then she'll have realized you're a hypocrite and a slut, if you don't mind my saying so, and she'll come to my arms and bring a case of beer and two ham pizzas. I invited her to come back whenever she liked, but I think she still hasn't heard the messages. On the other hand you, my darling Esmeralda, I know you're listening to this message as I leave it, your answering machine doesn't say you're not in but that you can't come to the phone. Do you know why you can't come to the phone? Because you're there with that retard who I'll bet went with you today to see a Meg Ryan picture, and it's not that I care, but you can be certain that even that retard hates Meg Ryan's movies and went only because he wants you to notice him, he wants to fill in the seventy-six centimeters that are free in your bed, it may even be Miki with his radish's sensibility, come to think of it, or maybe Angela, if she's decided to change her options. I'm not saying this to annoy you, it actually doesn't worry me at all, I want that clear, I'd just like to know so I won't bother him or her with my calls or spend too much money leaving them messages they won't answer because they're in bed with you commenting on Meg Ryan's latest movie while I talk only to answering machines and Scarlett O!, who tends not to answer because her mouth is full. I mean, once in a while it would be nice to talk to a human being for a change, even if it was you. You know? After all, I don't feel any rancor toward you and I'm not angry just because you behaved like a champion whore, but I really don't have the slightest interest in talking to you, and if you called me, do you know what I'd do? I'd hang up on you, Esmeralda, yeah, I'd hang up on you for being a whore, excuse my saying it to you this way, and even if you picked up the receiver right now I'd hang up immediately, not waiting for you to say my name or some insult or one of your criticisms like "immature" and those intellectual things you say, I wouldn't even invite you to watch the adult channel, even though at 3:45 they're showing "Desirée" and I know you would've liked it and it lasts only an hour and fifteen minutes, so in a short time we both could have raised our averages, at least I could have, because I don't know how your average is, I never think about you, and the sum total of nostalgia plus the joy of having freed myself from you is equal to zero, nothing, no feeling, I have a surplus of pizza and a deficit of loneliness, so as you can see, I'm calling only to tell you how good I'm feeling and how little I need to hear your voice. That's why I'm leaving this message so I won't have to hear you, but I'm going to stop now because the scene has begun where the black slave fucks the Union officer on the horse, and that's interesting because the officer has only one fuck in the whole movie, which is exactly one more than I've had in the two marvelous weeks without you. Don't bother to get back to me, I'll have the answering machine on for you, for Miki, for Angela, maybe I'll go out at night and call myself and leave a message because, really, now I'm free and can do whatever I want after the movie I didn't go to, and of all the possibilities, the only one I don't intend to do is talk to you. Bye, Esmeralda, and I hope a horse gives it to you up the ass.

(415) 952–3144

2:15 AM

— Hi. This is Conchita.

— Hi, Conchita.

— Mmmmhhh…You have a real man's voice.

— Oh, Conchita, I love talking to you. You always…make me feel good, you know?

— Always?

— Always…Well, you know who this is, don't you?

— Sure, you're a volcano…

— Oh, you must say that to everybody.

— Just to you, tiger…

— *Rrroooaoooorrr*…Oh, Conchita…

— Oh…

— I was calling all night but your line was busy…Did you work a lot?

— A little, yeah…What would you like to do today?

— Well, I don't know…whatever you think would be good, I guess.

— Where are you?

— In my office. They changed my coffee machine. I'd been

asking for it for a while, and finally…I was masterful, I think.

— How nice. Well, imagine a saxophone playing, and I begin to dance and take off my clothes around the coffee machine. Can you hear the music…and see me?

— It's just that…the machine is very small now and it's on top of the filing cabinet…I don't know whether you can dance there, it's a little cramped…

— Then I'll dance on you, I'll sit on your legs and slowly take off my blouse and my tight leather pants…

— All right, leave them on the armchair so they don't get wrinkled…

— I'll toss them on the floor, I'm so hot I don't have time to…

— Not on the floor…I mean…you might forget an article of clothing or I might move in my chair and roll over them, you know?

— …Wherever you want, all I'm thinking about is opening your fly and kneeling in front of you…

— Wait, let me move back a little…you might…

— Like this?

— That's it, better…

— I mean, do you like it?

— Oh, yeah…

— …

— Do I like what?

— My sucking you off.

— You're…?

— Yeah, well, I thought you'd like it and…

— Oh, yeah, I love it…

— Aha.

— Yeah.

— Now I move my tongue up and down, from your balls to the tip, it's so big…

— Seriously? And I didn't even…

— Didn't what?

— It's just that…

— Come on, tiger. What is it?

— Nothing, I tell you, just funny ideas of mine…

— You don't want to…

— I don't want to bother you…

— … share them with me?

— It's just that…

— What?

— Well, I don't want you to think I'm sick or anything but…

— You want rough sex?

— Really…

— Sodomy?

— Well…

— I can urinate on you…

— …

— Zoophilia? Necrophilia? Want me to be a paralyzed little girl?

— I only…only…want you to caress my head.

— Mmmhhh, sure, now I touch the tip gently with my fingertips and I…

— No, my other head. The one on my shoulders, I mean.

— You don't want…

— Just my head.

— Ah.

— Does that bother you?

— No, touching you always excites me.

— Thanks, a little lower, please, on the back of my neck.

— Like this?

— Oh, Conchita, you have such soft hands…

— Right.

— I hope I'm not bothering you…

— No, it's nothing.

— …I mean, you're used to other things…I hope I'm…

— Don't worry.

— Can you…

— What?

— You won't laugh?

— Of course not, I want you so much…I want your come running down my…

— Can you call me "kiddo?"

— What?

— "Kiddo"…it's just…I like…

— Kiddo?

— Ahhh…It sounds so good when you say it…I think there's something very special between us, Conchita.

— Sure.

— Really? Do you really think so?

— Yeah, sure, you're all man and I need you so much that…

— Oh, how nice that you think so…I…was afraid you wouldn't feel the same way, you know?

— Oh, kiddo…

— Oh, Conchita…come…give me your hand…that's it…

— …

— …

— And?

— And what, Conchita?

— Are we going…I mean…Are we going to stay like this?

— Do you like it?

— Well…it's…a little unusual…

— It's special.

— Right.

— Conchita…

— It's just that my boss, you know? If he walks past and I'm not saying anything…

— Oh, I understand.

— …Well he—he'll think it's a personal call or something…

— But it is.

— It is?

— Yes. I love you, Conchita.

— Aha.

— Really. I love you.

— Brilliant.

— …I've never found anybody who understands me like you do…Never.

— Kiddo…I don't know if…

— Do you want to marry me, Conchita?

— I'm already married, but sure I want to.

— Brilliant.

— Yeah.

— Well.

— Listen, my shift is over…Will you call me again?

— Sure, Conchita. We're married now.

— We are?

— Yeah.

— How nice.

— Yeah.

— Well. Bye.

— Bye-bye, darling.

(415) 952–3148

3:15 PM

— Yes?

— Don?

— Reginaldo?

— I saw the girl…

— You mean…

— Mary…

— Right. Well, you see, I'm with a client right now and…

— You have more important things to do? Is that what you're saying?

— Oh, no, no, no, it's just that…well, I wasn't expecting this call…

— …I thought you'd be interested in knowing…

— Really, I'm not.

— Did you ask her out to dinner?

— We haven't spoken, you know, the…

— It's a detail.

— …the job and…

— I try to give my clients, I don't know, satisfactory service. You know?

— Can I call you later?

— I'm looking at her right now. Her hair isn't so long.

— She said she would cut it. Surely by now…listen…

— And her nipples seem, you know, tiny, like two little dots.

— …my client…

— I say that because the man she's with is looking at them with no shame.

— Man?

— It almost looks like he's going to bury his…

— What man?

— …his lips between her breasts.

— But…

— Don't worry, he looks like a nice guy. He must really love her, he's kissing her with…with sincere love.

— Listen, I want to look at that detail in the contract more carefully. Right now I'm excusing myself for a few seconds, and I'm walking down the hall to the bathroom…

— You don't have to describe the whole building to me, Don.

— Now I'm in the bathroom, I check all the stalls, nobody's here WHAT MAN!? Shit.

— Hey, Don, you don't have to get so…

— And how do you want me to get? Huh? How do you want me to get with that bitch?

— It's just…

— A bitch!

— She's having a little fun. You have a wife, don't you?

— That has nothing to do with it, Reginaldo, nothing.

— Maybe it's not so bad…

— What isn't so bad? What do you mean isn't so bad?

— Well, maybe…it fits into your plans, right? I mean…

— You mean what?

— You wanted to be free of her, now you have a reason to leave her. Understand? She cheated on you, you leave her, everybody's even.

— Everybody's even.

— Everybody's even, exactly.

— But what kind of…

— You have to be compassionate, Don.

— What kind of a fucking killer are you? I mean…

— Don, don't get angry with me…

— Don't get…? I pay to…and now you tell me this shit about being compassionate! What do you do with your victims? Do you ask them out for fruit juice? Do you pay for their psychologist?

— …You're taking this too much to heart, Don, you have…

— Too much to heart, right, maybe the four of us could sit down and talk about it over tea and cakes…

— …you have an attitude problem.

— I'm sorry, this bathroom is closed! It can't be used right now because of alterations…

— What are you…

— …Yeah, within the hour, thanks, see you later…I was talking to a guy who wanted to come into the bathroom…

— You're monopolizing the bathroom, Don? You're really very egotistical. Do you know that?

— Right.

— So this is what we'll do: I'll return your advance and you'll break up with her, OK? And that's it.

— That's it.

— You have to get all that hate out of your heart, Don. It's poison.

— I'll tell you how…I'll tell you what we're going to do. I'll double the advance and I want you to kill him too.

— Him?

— Yeah, him! I want you to blow away his head! And his lips! And his balls! And everything that's touched Mary!

— But if that…

— Didn't you hear me?

— But if that poor guy has no idea, he's a dumb…

— Well let him die for being dumb!

— Oh, Don. I'm disappointed in how lightly you take this business. Do you think…

— For being dumb!

— Do you think you can deposit a sum of money in an account and that's it, they just disappear…

— Kill him!

— Don, could we keep the conversation elevated? I…

— Oh, shit, I think I've hired fucking Mother Teresa…

— Don…

— What do you want?

— Are you listening to me?

— Wait a minute, they're knocking on the door.

— Right.

— …

— …

— Reginaldo?

— Yeah?

— Tell me…tell me something. Where are they?

— In a restaurant, one of those…terraces…she…she's drinking mineral water and he's having a beer.

— Does she have a mobile phone?

— Do you mean a cell phone?

— Yeah, yeah, yeah, a cell phone!

— No, actually not.

— Are you sure?

— Absolutely.

— Neither one, no cell phone.

— No cell phone.

— How strange, because at this very moment Mary is calling me on the other line, Reginaldo.

— On the other…

— Yeah…

— Oh.

— Do you know what that means?

— Well I…

— Do you know what it means?

— What?

— That you're following some dimwit who isn't my girlfriend. Moron!

— Oh, Don, I can explain everything…it's just that…

— It's just what!?

— Well, the truth is I'm not looking at a restaurant, Don. And I'm not looking at her either…

— Right.

— I mean, she's at home and…

— And?

— …And I haven't seen any man or anything…

— Then what…

— I'm not saying she isn't going out with somebody, maybe she is, right?…

— Sure.

— …But I'm not aware of it.

— Then what are you a…

— Well, Don, I…I've been watching her for two days and…

— And how does that concern…

— Take it easy, Don…It's a long story.

— Summarize.

— Well, I stick with her day and night, day and night, you know? Waiting for…

— The moment.

— The moment, yeah.

— Right.

— And I'm there in my car listening to Bob Marley. You like Bob Marley?

— What does that have to do with…

— Well Bob Marley's on and I'm alone there in the car, you know? In the morning…

— Aha.

— And both mornings she's gone out in the morning to the bakery and…

— And you haven't…

— …And she's bought two butter croissants. You know? The kind that…

— Have butter, yeah…

— Two.

— Aha.

— And when she does…well…when she does she crouches in front of the baker's counter and chooses them carefully, as if she were choosing, I don't know, sheets or something… pointing at them one by one and then choosing the shiniest ones, and sometimes, the ones filled with chocolate…

— And Bob Marley. Shit.

— Wait, I'm almost finished. And then I said to myself… well…

— Come on, Reginaldo…

— Well…seeing her there, crouching in front of the croissants…

— Like sheets, right?

— Like sheets, yeah, I said to myself…Hey, Reginaldo! That's the girl for you.

— What?

— Yeah. Hey Reginaldo! That's the girl…you know?

— …

— …

— Hey, Reginaldo.

— And well, yeah…I thought that…maybe…if you don't love her…she and I could…

— See each other sometimes…

— See each other sometimes…

— Have a relationship…

— Yeah, that's right, have a relationship…

— Maybe one day have a couple of kids, huh?

— Ha, ha, a couple, yeah…

— And all because of croissants.

— All…

— Like sheets.

— Yeah.

— But really, are you an imbecile or what?

— Me?

— I paid you to…and you've…

— It's just that…

— You're an imbecile!

— Right.

— Well listen to me carefully, Reginaldo. Either you do your job or I'll have to hire somebody else to take care of you. And I promise you he won't fall in love! Do you hear me?

— Yeah.

— He'll tear off your balls and Mary's tits!

— And if I only give her a scare…like "if I see you again, blah, blah, blah…" and like that…

— Your balls!

— Sure.

— So I want the job finished by tomorrow, or I'll finish with you before Monday.

— OK.

— It's harsh but that's the way it is, OK?

— OK.

— I mean, I'm not a monster or anything… I picked her up. Remember?

— Yeah, she must be grateful…

— Tonight. Is that clear?

— Tonight, yeah.

— If not, balls.

— Yeah, understood.

— Bye.

— Bye-bye.

(415) 496–6642

8:45 ᴀᴍ

— Hello, this is Esmeralda. I can't come to the phone right now, but leave your message and your number after the tone and I'll get back to you as soon as I can. Ciao.

— I…think I…I got carried away and called you…Well, I guess you've listened to it by now…Though maybe not, because Miki and Angela haven't listened to the messages I left them yet, people don't listen sometimes, other people's words upset them as if they were, I don't know, fake tickets for an opening, or checks with insufficient funds—you give the check to the cashier and he gives you no money in return… Sometimes people even listen to their messages and they say "all right, I'll return that call," that's how they say it, calmly, finishing their coffee and the newspaper, the check's being processed, but then they don't call back. The message sits in the machine all alone, hoping another arrives to keep it company. I wonder if they can see or hear one another while the person finishes his coffee and his newspaper and that takes days and days, they're the longest coffee and newspaper in the world, but…but…well, the most likely thing is that you heard the message already, I guess, though maybe not, because you never get up early in the morning, which was sometimes a little annoying. A person wanted to go out for breakfast and you were dead to the world, there was no way to wake you, sometimes it was intolerable, if you don't mind my saying so, but sometimes it was brilliant— with your eyes half-opened and your face buried in my chest like a kitten, you know? And if I tried to move, you took my arm and put it around you, put my face against your neck, you were asleep and wouldn't let me move because I kept you warm, that's what you said, like a kitten. I'm not saying you're an animal, of course, don't take it that way, it was nice, not only that, it was incredible, but what if I think that maybe you didn't listen to my message because maybe you're there with another guy, right? And it's not that it bothers me, I think you have the right, I'd be with other girls if I could, you know? It's just that I don't know, I mean if you're with another guy and last night you saw some movie with Meg Ryan, well, it's possible you haven't had time to listen to my message, that you're still like a kitten with your neck buried in his chest instead of mine and his face instead of mine pressing against your hair, I think it's the most natural thing, I'm not reproaching you, not at all, I don't even mean that it actually happened. I mean, really, it's only a manner of speaking, maybe you didn't listen to my message because your answering machine has a peculiar system, or it amuses you to listen to messages in a different order, or the previous tape broke, you never know, right? Or maybe you're there with your coffee and paper or just with your coffee because he has the paper and you're thinking you'll return the call later and well, anything can happen, I mean for example, one day you have a girlfriend you adore and love and the next day, not knowing why, you don't have anything anymore, nobody loves you or takes your arm to put it around her waist and you spend the nights counting things in front of the adult channel…No, that's not a good example. It's all the same, I mean, you know? What I'm trying to say is maybe it's better if you haven't listened to the message, but you can do what you want, right? But in principle I'd ask you please not necessarily to listen to that message, I mean, this one yes, this one's fine, isn't it? This is a good message after all because I'm not reproaching you at all for the bastard who slept with you, so you can listen to this one but not the earlier one, OK? Maybe it would be better, you know? Just not to complicate things more, because it's not that it matters to me, really, it's just that I think you and I are both people who are…uuuhh…mature, that's right, mature, and we shouldn't…you know…do things like that…make calls like that…I wouldn't like to come home one day and find a message like the one I left you, it would be nice to receive a message sometimes, but maybe afterward I'd say "shit"— forgive the language, Esmeralda—"shit, that call wasn't so nice. It was a shitty call," though I made it with no desire to offend, right? In fact, everything I said was the absolute truth, but I think maybe, I don't know, maybe I shouldn't say it that way, maybe the best thing would be to ask you out for coffee, for example, that's mature, and tell you in person that I think you're a whore, but say it in person, right? This way at least you couldn't do what you're doing now, with your coffee and paper, listening to the call with the son of a bitch you slept with last night, because in spite of the fact that this call has good intentions, you should know that I know the two of you are laughing at my message and thinking "well, I'll return the call soon," and it hurts me deeply to think that, Esmeralda, because it seems to me that two weeks of separation isn't enough time for you to go to bed with the first guy who comes along, to be perfectly frank, I hoped you'd at least have a little sensitivity and be in mourning or something, I don't know, a couple of months would've been enough, it would've given me time to start ordering sushi instead of pizza, for example, you know? Or to watch some documentary instead of movies on the adult channel that I already know by heart, I don't know, something, but two weeks is very sad, not because of me because it's all the same to me, but because of you, because it means, if you think about it, that you feel so lonely without me that you need somebody to fill up the space in your bed, as well as the nine-hundred-square-centimeter area of the breakfast chair, and the twelve hundred that are free in the shower, and above all, the roughly thousand cubic centimeters your arm leaves free on your body when there's not another arm to go around your waist, and the four hectares of my heart that are empty now. But that's your problem, I don't want to get involved in your life, understand? Even though your life is really pathetic with that bastard who went to see Meg Ryan in order to spend the night with you, it's your life and that must be respected, right? Maybe one day you'll reconsider and realize that the only man who loved you in the way you deserve is me, but by then it'll be too late, a shame, and I'll be with another woman who'll curl up in bed so she won't have to open her eyes until I rest my head in her hair or nuzzle her cheek with my forehead, but do you know what you can do when that happens? You can leave me a message on my answering machine. You're bound to be destroyed, I imagine, because you'll have discovered that you love me like nobody else in the world, but you can cry, yeah, you can shed a few tears into the receiver, I'll be listening, you know, in my robe, with my coffee and all, and I'll try to hide the phone from the girl I spent the night with so she won't be scared away, I'll tell her to take a shower or something, then I'll take the pizza boxes off the telephone and raise the volume on the answering machine, trying to hear your tears falling on the receiver. That'll be a difficult moment, because she'll come out of the shower and want to know where the shampoo is and almost hear you, but I'll lower the volume in time and show her the cabinet under the sink, where you kept your sanitary napkins. Then I'll go back to the phone and keep listening, because by then you'll be sobbing desperately for me to come back to you, that you can't live without me. And you'll move me, I don't deny it. You'll make me feel very sad. I'll remember, you know? I'll remember when we had breakfast together and when we went to the country, I'll remember all that. I'll even remember some things that never happened, like when we fucked in an elevator with a view of the city, remember? Of course you don't remember because it didn't happen, but I do. And it was brilliant. And it'll be brilliant thinking about nothing but that fuck we didn't have—because the ones we did have, Esmeralda, let's be frank, weren't anything special—and I'll sit in front of the phone alone, very alone, the way you feel now, and very small, yeah, that's true, and without thinking about the girl I've left in the bathroom washing her hair with a shampoo she took from your cabinet of sanitary napkins, I'll get dressed, and not saying anything to the poor girl, I'll leave and run to your house and ring your bell. I'll stand there for a few minutes until you come to the door, because you'll be so shattered you won't want to talk to anybody and you'll go to the door only when you think the bell's about to explode and you'll see me there. I'll look handsome standing there, my fly still open—not *already* open, Esmeralda, but *still* open—and my shirt half unbuttoned, my hair uncombed and my face swollen with sleep. And you'll look radiant to me, with your red eyes and messy hair, pizza boxes and beer bottles all over the floor, bottles, because you wouldn't drink from a can. And we'll stare at each other, and do you know what I'll say to you? Want to know? I'll say "whore!" Yeah, that's what I'll say to you, I'll say "whore!" approximately twenty-two times, because at first you won't understand what's going on, then you'll try to answer but won't be able to because I'll keep shouting whore-whore-whore-whore-whore-whore-whore-whore-whore-whore-whore-whore-whore-whore-whore-whore-whore-whore-whore until you close the door and start to cry again because you've lost me forever. Then call the imbecile who slept with you! Just call him! You're sure to reach his machine and you'll repeat everything you told me and he'll do what I did and then go back home where a girl fresh out of the shower will be waiting for him, and she'll ask "what happened?" and he'll put a loaf of multigrain bread on the table that he bought on the way and say "for breakfast" and nothing will have happened there, only in your house will something have happened that nobody will remember but will remain forever on our answering machines like a check with insufficient funds, like a blown kiss carried away by the wind, like a whore at the end of the street who not even the poorest customers approach......... I've gone on long enough, I only wanted to tell you not to listen to that message. After all, I loved you a lot, once, and in no way would I like us to end up angry, and I promise not to call you a whore when I run into you on the street with one of those men, because it's normal and I don't reproach you, that would be inconsiderate on my part because by then you'll know how much of a whore you are and how you lost the chance for the man of your life who loved you so much. Bye.

(415) 952–3144

12:14 AM

— Hello?

— Conchita?

— Mmmmmhhh…you have a real ma…

— I've spent four hours trying to reach you, Conchita.

— Oh, I've been wanting you too…What di…

— Don't lie to me!

— Oh daddy, you sound so strong…Do you want to hurt me? Huh? Do you want to hit me?

— Yes!…Well…not so much…I don't…

— I love to be hit on the butt.

— Ah, yeah?

— Ohhhh, yeah…

— Ah…Well then…I won't hit you!

— Please, please, beat me…

— No!

— Mmmhh…how you make me suffer…

— I know, Conchita. But I think you've earned it. I mean… four hours, you know?

— All that time just to talk to me?

— Yeah, and the operator offered me other girls but I…

— Aaahh…

— …But I tried to explain our thing to her, you know?

— Yeeeeaah…

— I think you ought to…ought to explain to her that you and I… I mean, to avoid misunderstandings.

— Where are you?

— Oh. In my office, I…decided to put the file cabinet next to the door, see? So you can dance behind the desk…

— On top of you?

— I knew you'd like that.

— I like you.

— And I like you, Conchita.

— I want to taste your come in my mouth.

— Oh, Conchita, I don't know if we ought…

— Please…

— It's just that now…well…I don't know…I'd feel…I wouldn't feel like something special, you know? It isn't…

— Special?

— Marriage always…cools these things off a little…

— You don't like your wife, do you?

— Oh, no, she's terrific, she's the best…I didn't mean…

— And what would make you feel…special?

— Well…since you mentioned it…maybe…

— Now I'm lowering your trousers…

— Conchita, please, I'm trying to have a conversation…

— Can I talk with my mouth full?

— Conchita…Conchita no…Conchita!

— Is something wrong?

— Yeah, Conchita, I want you to stop.

— Right.

— Did you stop yet?

— Yeah, I suppose so.

— Now, listen to me. I know you love your career and that you're a professional...

— ...

— ...it's just that, you know? It isn't easy...oh, shit, I've always been terrible with words...

— Don't say that.

— Of course I am! It's like...like they bounced, you know? Like fake tickets to an opening or checks with insufficient funds....I either can't say them or nobody wants to hear them or...

— I hear you. Now I want to hear you moan...

— No! Do you see what I'm talking about, Conchita? Do you understand? There are so many moans, snorts, noises, so many things a person can do with his mouth, words...are like... the least important...I don't know...

— You and I don't need words, tiger...

— ...and you...talk to so many people...men, I mean... they're...I feel...

— Men.

— Yeah...

— But you're the only one who...

— Stop lying to me! Oh, I'm sorry Conchita...I...didn't mean to shout at you. You understand me, don't you? Do you understand how I feel?

— The truth is...

— I'd like…oohh…I'd like you to…well…I'm in this office all the time with this coffee machine and the green file cabinet, you know? I hate that fucking green file cabinet, Conchita! I hate the coffee machine! You know?

— You hate the coffee machine.

— I hate it, yeah. It's lousy coffee, and I lied to you, they haven't changed it, and I didn't move the file cabinet either… I'm sorry, Conchita. I wanted to impress you, but the fact is that everything's the same, everything in my miserable life is the same…

— You have me…

— That's just it! I don't have you, Conchita! I have you like everybody else has you! I'm in my filthy office and you're… you're…talking to all of them…

— Sure…

— I can't even go to the bathroom, you know? There's an… an old guy, an executive or something…every time I go in the bathroom he's there talking on the phone…

— An executive.

— Saying strange things…I don't know…and he throws me out, he throws me out of the bathroom, Conchita!

— Maybe…there's another bathroom you can go to or…

— I have to go to the café, Conchita. I go downstairs, go to the café, order a coffee just to order something, and I go to the bathroom, I leave the coffee without tasting it, I pay, and I go back to my office…

— Yeah, it's sad.

— It's sad.

— And what…and how can I…

— I want you to leave that job, Conchita. That's…that's what I want.

— My job?

— It's difficult to bear…maybe…maybe in the café next door they need a waitress and then you could…you could serve me coffee, you know, and then I'll go to the bathroom and you'll know there's an executive in the office bathroom saying strange things on the phone. It'll be fun…

— You want me to quit my job.

— Exactly, yeah. I knew you'd understand. You're smart, Conchita. Very smart. That's why we get along so well.

— And why should…why should I…

— For us, you know? For…our thing.

— But, let's see, who the hell are you?

— Don't you know who I am, Conchita?

— It's just that…Do I know you?

— Don't you know who the hell I am, Conchita?

— Reginaldo? You're Reginaldo, right? Only you…these jokes only occur to…

— Conchita, I thought there was something special between us.

— Aren't you…

— You said that…

— Regi…

— You said we had something special!

— Excuse me, it's just that…

— We got married! Do you remember? Shit, I married you!

— We…

— Oh, shit.

— I…

— You don't even…

— Look…

— Shit.

— Listen, I can give you a blow job, OK? You'll see how much good it'll do you. A blow job and like new…

— No, it's too late.

— It won't take any…

— It's too late, Conchita. There's nothing…nothing more to do, understand?

— I…

— Don't say anything. It's just that I don't think…I don't think our thing is working.

— Maybe…

— It's no use. Please, don't insist, OK? It's better to leave things as they are. It's…

— Right.

— …less painful, right?

— Yeah, sure.

— All right.

— All right.

— Bye, Conchita.

— Will you call me again?

— I don't know, Conchita. I honestly don't know.

— Can I do anything for you?

— No, I don't think so. It was nice while it lasted, wasn't it?

— It was, yeah.

— Can you call me "kiddo"? "Bye, kiddo"?

— Bye, kiddo.

— Thanks, Conchita. Bye.

— Bye-bye.

(415) 937–0353

11:31 AM

— Welcome to our customer service center. If you need information regarding any of our products, press 1. For questions about bills and fees, press 2. If you...

2

— One moment, please. We're here to serve you better. Taaaa-ta-ta-taaa-ta-ta-ta-ta-ra-ra-raaaa-tiiiii-ti-ti-tiiii-taa-ra-ra-ra-ra-ra-ta-ra-ra-taaaa-ta-ta-ta-raaaa-tu-ri-ru-taaaa-ta-ta-taaaa-ta-ta-ta-ra-ra-raaaa-tiiiii-ti-ti-tiiii-taa-ra-ra-ra-ra-ra-ta-ra-ra-taaaa-ta-ta-ta-raaaa-tu-ri-ru-taaaa-ta-ta-taaaa-ta-ta-ta-ra-ra-raaaa-tiiiii-ti-ti-tiiii-taa-ra-ra-ra-ra-ra-ta-ra-ra-taaaa-ta-ta-ta-raaaa-tu-ri-ru-taaaa-ta-ta-taaaata-ta-ta-ra-ra-raaaa-tiiiii-ti-ti-tiiii-taa-ra-ra-ra-ra-ra—ta-ra-ra-taaaa-ta-ta-ta-raaaa-tu-ri-ru-ta-aaa-ta-ta-taaaa-ta-ta-ta-ra-ra-raaaa-tiiiii-ti-ti-tiiii-taa-ra-ra-ra-ra-ra-ta-ra-ra-taaaa-ta-ta-ta-raaaa-tu-ri-ru- This is Debi. How may I help you?

— I'd like to speak to the sales representative Jorge, please.

— One moment please. We're here to serve you better. Taaaa-ta-ta-taaaa-ta-ta-ta-ta-ra-ra-raaaa-tiiiii-ti-ti-tiiii-

81

taa-ra-ra-ra-ra-ra-ta-ra-ra-taaaa-ta-ta-ta-raaaa-tu-ri-ru-taaaa-ta-ta-taaaa-ta-ta-ta-ra-ra-raaaa-tiiiii-ti-ti-tiiii-taara-ra-ra-ra-ra-ta-ra-ra-taaaa-ta-ta-ta-raaaa-tu-ri-ru-taaaa-ta-ta-taaaa-ta-ta-ta-ta-ra-ra-raaaatiiiii-ti-ti-tiiii-taa-ra-ra-ra-ra-ra-ta-ra-ra-taaaa-ta-ta-ta-raaaa-tu-ri-ru-taaaa-ta-ta-taaaa-ta-ta-ta-ta-ra-ra-raaaa-tiiiii-ti-ti-tiiii-taa-ra-ra-ra-ra-ra-ta-ra-ra-taaaa-ta-ta-ta-raaaa-tu-ri-ru-taaaa-ta-ta-taaaa-ta-ta-ta-ta-ra-ra-raaaa-tiiiii-ti-ti-tiiii-raa-ra-ra-ra-ra-ra-ta-ra-ra-taaaa-ta-ta-ta-raaaa-tu-ri-ru- This is Jorge. How may I help you?

— This is Godínez. X-3459362-Y.

— How may I help you, Señor Godínez?

— I want to cancel my contract.

— Cancel.

— Yes, I found a better contract with another company and…I want to stop using your service.

— No problem, sir. Let me see…

— I don't want anything more to do with you, understand?

— Of course, Señor…Godínez, right?

— Exactly. Can you cancel it right now?

— I only have to find your file and then…

— I detest all of you.

— Excuse me?

— I hate you. I don't want another cent of my money to end up in your pockets or pay any of your salaries. Is that clear?

— Perfectly, sir. I have it…

— You're the most repulsive people I've ever encountered, you're garbage, you're dog shit smeared on the sole of my shoe…

— I'm sorry, sir, but we can't cancel you.

— Ca…

— It shows here that you have an outstanding transaction. Godínez…transaction. Yes.

— Transaction? But wh…?

— It's a complaint about double billing.

— Right.

— It's been filed but isn't resolved.

— I filed it!

— That's right, sir.

— Well I'm unfiling it.

— That isn't possible, sir. Otherwise anyone could…

— I have to resolve it.

— You have to resolve it.

— But how…

— I'm sorry, sir.

— Let me see, let me take a breath…now, how can I resolve it?

— You have to send the original and a copy of your bills to Palomares 5, 6C, accompanied by a written complaint and a certificate of ownership of the property…

— The owner lives in Sudan!

— Oh…I'm sorry, sir.

— Can't you cancel my contract?

— Well, you can bring a notarized letter from the owner saying that in fact you lived there, certified by a Sudanese notary, authenticated at the embassy, and translated by a certified translator into…

— You sons of bitches! Crooked sons of bitches! Did you

hear me? Are you…?

— Perfectly, sir.

— Shits! That's what you are! Shits!

— I'm sorry, sir. Do you have any other question?

— What?

— This is the customer service center, sir. You're a customer. Do you need service?

Click.

— Señor Godínez…Señor Godínez?

(415) 952–3148

1:53 P.M

— Yes?

— Don?

— What? Is it over?

— No.

— Fuck y…

— I thought maybe you'd be calmer now and we could talk about all that "if I see you again blah, blah, blah…"

— Shit no! I want you to go in that house right now and do your job!

— She… she's pretty, isn't she?

— Yeah. She was.

— It won't be easy.

— It'll hurt me more than it hurts you, Reginaldo. You can't imagine.

— I hope she doesn't have time to see me, because if she looks at me with those eyes…

— It's your balls that are at risk.

— Right. Don't worry. I'm a professional before anything else. I'll do it…

— Call me when you finish, OK?

— …I'll do it tonight.

— Call me when you finish, OK? I'll be at home.

— In your house.

— At home, yeah.

— OK.

(415) 496–6642
5:26 P.M

— Hello, this is Esmeralda. I can't come to the phone right now, but leave your message and your number after the tone and I'll get back to you as soon as I can. Ciao.

— Esmeralda, I'm going to kill myself. I…I've thought it over carefully and…well, yesterday I saw a movie that wasn't on the adult channel, you know? The last few weeks I've counted, and I've seen fifty-six-and-a-half movies on the adult channel and yesterday I asked myself, why not watch something else? I mean, I had pizza and beer and all and I said to myself why not watch something else? Maybe my right hand is tired of being with me because it seems everybody is tired of being with me and, of course, it shouldn't be used for everything a person sees fit, even though it's my right hand, you know? It's a joke, "my right hand" and all… anyway…the fact is I saw a movie that maybe you'd have liked because it's French, right? And it's a little intellectual, like you, and besides you liked "French Kiss," so I don't know, I thought maybe you'd have liked the movie even though Meg Ryan wasn't in it or anything, but there were two girls,

87

one of the actresses was pretty but nobody has heard of her. She's French or something and nobody knows her. In the movie, one girl was good and happy, the other one not, but she was the pretty one, and in the end the pretty one commits suicide, she jumps out a window. I didn't see what floor it was, but it must have been very high because she died. Well, they didn't show her corpse or anything, and nobody said "damn it, she died," but I understood that she did die because she didn't appear again and then the movie was over. And I thought "what the hell, that would be good." Not that it would be good to jump, of course, because maybe you'd fall on the roof of a car and not really die, or on the electric cables and bounce and then fall on the roof of a car and not really die, but it would be good, you know? to kill yourself. There'd be no more pizza or beer or adult channel, but women wouldn't leave you either, right? I mean, they couldn't because you'd be dead, I've never heard of leaving a dead man, maybe the body, yeah, well, you can forget about it or leave it in formaldehyde to preserve it, but the man himself you can't leave him any more. Because he's dead. And if I called somebody on the phone, they couldn't not answer the call because I'm dead, I mean, they'd say "shit, he's dead, how can he make a call?" and they'd call right back, with their coffee in their hand, not finishing the paper, though maybe they wouldn't know where to call because, well, I've never known the number of a dead man, have you? So I thought "well, so I'd die and be on to something else" and then I wanted to tell you so you'd know, maybe you'd be interested in knowing, because after all you'd be a little bit to blame, right? I mean, everybody would say "And why the devil did he die?" and the others would say "it was Esmeralda's fault," and if you went to my funeral they'd give you awful looks. Of course you'd have to go, because after all we loved each other a lot for four Meg Ryan movies, but people would still give you awful looks and point at you, Esmeralda, and you'd feel very bad, so that bastard you spend your nights with would leave you because he couldn't stand seeing you cry so much for another man, maybe you don't understand it, maybe it's a male thing, but you can be jealous of a dead man. Though everybody would be pointing a finger at the bastard and saying "there's the bastard who's dating the girlfriend who's to blame for the dead man dying," it wouldn't be easy for him, and you should think about that poor man, after all, he's not to blame for anything, I mean, he's a real son of a bitch but he's not to blame, right? I don't reproach him at all for that, but once I've killed myself, everybody will reproach him, yeah, even that dimwit Miki and that snob Angela will reproach him. In short, I'm telling you so you can be prepared, right? because afterward you're the last one who'll find out and I have a high opinion of you, Esmeralda, you're a lecherous whore but I still have a high opinion of you and wanted you to be the first to know. So if you feel very bad about what you've done to me, you can still run out to the street, half-dressed, and run to my house and ring the bell hoping you'll arrive in time because you never know, right? Maybe I'm busy slitting my wrists with a razor, that's elegant and doesn't make much noise, so if I don't open the door, it's not because I don't want to or because I've gone out to buy more beer but only because I'm bleeding to death in the bathtub with the razor in my hand, and of course, looking like that, you can't be a good host. If I do that, I'll leave keys for you with my neighbor so you won't have to knock down the door because, obviously, with that tiny sweet body that curls up like a kitten, you couldn't even scratch the door, and I'd still be there inside losing blood while you'd be shouting outside for me to let you in, as if I could, sure, you've always thought I ought to do whatever you wanted even if I'm bleeding to death in a bathtub, that's why I left you, but even so, I didn't call to remind you of your mistakes, only to let you know what you should do. I mean, because it's a good idea to be prepared. I've also been thinking about hanging myself, I mean, it's a little unpleasant, but it's kind of classic, hanging yourself from a beam and all, the problem is I don't have beams at home. I was thinking that you have a balcony that could be used as a beam, I mean, it's metal and isn't going to fall or anything, but I suppose you wouldn't let me use it because you're an egotistical shit. Yeah, Esmeralda, I didn't want to tell you, but it's time you knew you're an egotistical shit, and it makes me very sad because I respect you, but it's true, so I won't ask you for your fucking balcony or your understanding or that you curl up with your eyes half-closed with my face in your hair, I won't ask you for shit so you'll get fucked up, and after my death you'll feel worse for not even letting me use your balcony, even though you never use it, I know because I've slept at your house a lot more than that bastard who sleeps there now, who probably hasn't even realized there's a balcony, I've slept there six hundred fifty-four nights,

I counted, so you see I know, and I'm not even counting fucking in the middle of the afternoon or the times I've gone there alone to eat supper or when I went up just to use the bathroom, no, I'm talking about whole nights when I slept there and got up there and caused an estimated twenty-two percent increase in your electric bill and thirty-one percent in your water bill and we never, you hear me? never! used that damn balcony that you won't let me use but in any case it doesn't matter, I didn't even want it, after all I can kill myself in thousands of ways, I can…well, I can…I could stay in a garage inside a car with the motor running, of course, I'd have to get a car. Don't think it's cheap to kill yourself, I mean, if you do it like the girl in the movie it's free, but you also need a high apartment, and they're more expensive, you know? and of course you fucked over the person who co-signed your lease, you did, because who'll pay for the months that are left, and I don't want to get involved in anybody's problems, I already have enough problems here alone and abandoned by my long-time girlfriend to create problems for other people who aren't to blame for your being an out-and-out whore, I mean, excuse me but it's true, you know? I'd rather not beat around the bush so afterward you can't say I lied to you or something. In any case, I don't want you to take my death personally, all right? I mean, it's true that your leaving me and your egotistical attitude will be the main cause of my sad decision, but, I don't know, there are other things, I mean, a person doesn't kill himself for just one reason, right? I mean, I guess not, because it seems to me it wouldn't be worth it to die because of you when you don't matter to me at all, but still you're the only reason I can think of. I don't know why the girl in the movie killed herself, for example, because I really didn't understand anything in the movie, just that at the end she jumped out the window. Well, I guess, in short… The fact is you shouldn't worry about me, the fact that you're the only cause I can think of for my premature death shouldn't make you feel guilty, OK? Well, bye.

(415) 496–6642

5:34 P.M

— Hello, this is Esmeralda. I can't come to the phone right now, but leave your message and your number after the tone and I'll get back to you as soon as I can. Ciao.

— Hello, it's me again…I only wanted to remind you that… well, that I'll leave you a key at my neighbor's in case you want…I mean, ummm, it makes no sense because you won't stop me, right? But it's always good…you know…Bye. Goodbye…forever, yeah…Goodbye.

(415) 937-0353

7:31 PM

— Welcome to our customer service center. If you need information about any of our products, press 1. To find out about bills and fees, press 2. If y…

2

— One moment please. We're here to serve you better. Ta-aaa-ta-ta-taaaa-ta-ta-ta-ta-ra-ra-raaaa-tiiiii-ti-ti-tiiii-taa-ra-ra-ra-ra-ra-ta-ra-ra-taaaa-ta-ta-ta-raaaa-tu-ri-ru-taaaa-ta-ta-taaaa-ta-ta-ta-ra-ra-raaaa-tiiiii-ti-ti-tiiii-taa-ra-ra-ra-ra-ra-ta-ra-ra-taaaa-ta-ta-ta-raaaa-tu-ri-ru-taaaa-ta-ta-taaaa-ta-ta-ta-ra-ra-raaaa-tiiiii-ti-ti-tiiii-taa-ra-ra-ra-ra-ra-ta-ra-ra-taaaa-ta-ta-ta-raaaa-tu-ri-ru-taaaa-ta-ta-taaaa-ta-ta-ta-ra-ra-raaaa-tiiiii-ti-ti-tiiii-taa-ra-ra-ra-ra-ra-ta-ra-ra-taaaa-ta-ta-ta-raaaa-tu-ri-ru-taaaa-ta-ta-taaaa-ta-ta-ta-ra-ra-raaaa-tiiiii-ti-ti-tiiii-taa-ra-ra-ra-ra-ra-ta-ra-ra-taaaa-ta-ta-ta-raaaa-tu-ri-ru This is Remi. How may I help you?

— I'd like to speak with the sales representative Jorge, please.

— One moment please. We're here to serve you better. Taaaa-ta-ta-taaaa-ta-ta-ta-ta-ra-ra-raaaa-tiiiii-ti-ti-tiiii-taa-ra-ra-ra-ra-ra-ta-ra-ra-taaaa-ta-ta-ta-raaaa-turi-ru-ta-aaa-ta-ta-taaaa-ta-ta-ta-ta-ra-ra-raaaa-tiiiii-ti-ti-tiiii-taaa-ra-ra-ra-ra-ra-ta-ra-ra-taaaa-ta-ta-ta-raaaa-tu-ri-ru-taaaa-ta-ta-taaaa-ta-ta-ta-ta-ra-ra-raaa-tiiiii-ti-ti-tiiii-taa-ra-ra-ra-ra-ra-ta-ra-ra-taaaa-ta-ta-ta-raaaa-tu-ri-ru-taaaa-ta-ta-taaaa-ta-ta-ta-ta-ra-ra-raaaa-tiiiii-ti-ti-tiiii-taa-ra-ra-ra-ra-ra-ta-ra-ra-taaaa-ta-ta-ta-raaaa-turi-ru-taaaa-ta-ta-taaaa-ta-ta-ta-ta-ra-ra-raaaa-tiiiii-ti-ti-tiiii-taaa-ra-ra-ra-ra-ra-ta-ra-ra-taaaa-ta-ta-ta-raaaa-tu-ri-ru- This is Jorge. How can I help you?

— This is Godínez. X-3459362-Y.

— How can I help you, Señor Godínez?

— Do you like your job, Jorge?

— Excuse me?

— Do you like your job?

— I'm sorry, sir. This is the customer…

— …"service center," I know. I'm a customer and need some service. I need to know if you like your job…

— Well…yes?

— Your office is all right?

— I have a coffee machine.

— A coffee machine, right.

— And a green file cabinet.

— Aha.

— And that's all, sir.

— That's all. Well I want you to know, Jorge, I want you to know that I'm going to kill you.

— Oh.

— I'm going to dig out your eyes with two spoons…

— Could you repeat your…

— And then I'm going to skin you with a razor.

— …your ID number, sir?

— So say goodbye to your fucking office, imbecile, because I'm going to…

— Your ID numb…

— …I'm going to eat your guts, do you hear me? …You hear me?

— Perfectly, sir.

— I'll dance on your grave, Jorge.

— I don't understand…

— I hope you die.

— Do you need assistance? You're a customer and this…

— Fuck you, Jorge.

— Delighted to be of service, sir.

(415) 937–1092

— Yes?

— Don.

— Shit. Haven't I told you not to call me at this number?

— No.

— I'm telling you now! Call me at the other one.

— What other one?

— The one you called me at in the afternoon, idiot! On this one anybody…anybody could…my wife could…

— I don't know if I remember that number…is it 21…

— Don't say that number on this number! Just call me.

— And how do I know if it's the number?

— If I don't answer, it isn't.

— And if you don't answer, where do I call you?

— …

— …

— Shit.

— You see.

— What a fuck-up. Then just tell me, yes or no?

— Yes. It's done.

— Ufff...I feel relieved. Don't you feel relieved, Reginaldo?

— One less weight on my shoulders.

— How...You know, how did you...?

— A handkerchief.

— OK...What a relief, huh?

— Yeah.

— You don't sound very relieved.

— I am, yeah.

— Right. And the body?

— The body?

— Yeah, shit, the body. It's in the contract: the body disappears.

— I have a contract?

— If they find the body...

— I had no idea about a con...

— ...I'll be the first one they...understand? They'll see her date book, the calls...

— The calls.

— What are you going to do with the body?

— I don't know. I left it there.

— "I don't know, I left it there."

— On the bed, like that.

— Listen: you're going to carry the body to the bathroom.

— The bathroom.

— The bathroom, yeah. Then you take the wide knife from the kitchen, the one that looks like a short ax. Have you seen it?

— No.

— It's in the knife drawer. You take it...

— Right.

— You take it and carry it to the bathroom…Then you cut her into pieces.

— Shit.

— Into pieces!

— All right.

— You go to the closet, right? There's a closet in her room.

— This is in the contract?

— In the closet there's a black suitcase, a big one, that's mine too. You put in the pieces, the ties, and two brown jackets…

— They'll get stained.

— Put them in!

— With the pieces.

— Exactly, with the pieces. You take out the suitcase…

— Her legs too?

— You take out the suitcase and carry it to the river…

— Her legs too?

— What too?!

— Do I cut them too into…

— Pieces, yeah.

— She had…she has nice legs.

— Oh, yeah, nice legs. And lips.

— I haven't seen her nipples. I'll look now.

— Reginaldo, don't be morbid, all right?

— Excuse me…it's just that…it's a shame, isn't it?

— Right. We'll miss her.

— Did you take her to…

— …you throw the suitcase in the river…

— Did you go to dinner?

— Yeah, we went.

— Was she happy?

— Yeah, very happy. Then you go home.

— I like to leave a client happy.

— Brilliant. Then you go home.

— I'd like…

— Make sure nobody follows you.

— …I'd like to have a drink, I mean, before I go home. This has been very…

— Have whatever you want, but first, the suitcase and the river.

— …very sad.

— Sure.

— …

— Reginaldo.

— Yeah?

— You did it, didn't you? I mean…what I asked you to do.

— The pieces.

— No before that. You took care…

— Yeah, sure.

— Sure?

— Well, I'm here, aren't I?

— She didn't look at you with those eyes…

— No.

— And then, "if I see you again, blah, blah, blah…"

— We didn't have time to talk. It's a shame.

— Listen, I'll call you.

— When?

— Now.

— Ah…What for?

— I'm going to call you at Mary's house, and if Mary answers the telephone, you can say goodbye to your balls, understand?

— I don't think she can…I mean, she's…

— That's what I hope.

— And if nobody answers?

— It's the same thing, idiot, because you have to be there and take care of the pieces, remember?

— Sure.

— Is that clear?

— And if…and if I answer?

— Then everything's fine.

— Everything's fine.

— Yeah.

— OK

— I'll call you then.

— OK.

— Bye.

— Bye-bye.

(415) 496–6642

4:23 AM

— Hello, this is Esmeralda. I can't come to the phone right now, but leave your…

Click.

— I'm here. I haven't found the knife you mentioned, but there's another one that'll work, one of those electric ones…

— So you're the imbecile.

— Don?

— …

— Don, is that you?

— My name isn't Don.

— Oh. Then…I think you…you have the wrong number…I mean, I'm here but…

— I know perfectly well where I'm calling, you son of a bitch. I've called this number many more times than you, to be exact, I've called it thirty-two times in the last two weeks. I counted.

— Oh…

— Do you want to know how many times I've slept there? Do you?

— Not really.

— Do you know what you are? Do you know what you are? You're jealous of me.

— Ah.

— Yeah, because you know I have been and am much more important than you in the life of that woman you're spending the night with.

— This wom…Listen, I'm not…

— No need to tell me stories, you piece of garbage. Do you think I don't know? I know perfectly well, I know everything.

— Everything.

— Everything.

— Well, I…I really tried to resist, you know? Tonight I called…

— I don't want to hear your story. Don't you understand? I don't care, it's irrelevant, even if I had a microscope that saw the tiniest bacteria, I couldn't find a reason to care about your stupid version of events.

— Did you say stupid?

— I said stupid, you pile of shit. What? Does it bother you?

— Did you say pile of shit?

— It looks like I'll have to kick you in your ears and clean them out, you bastard.

— I'd like to see that…

— You wouldn't even see it coming, moron. But I want to speak to the owner of this circus, not the baboon. Right now you pick up MY woman from the bed…

— She's not on the bed anymore, she's in the bathtub.

— You pick her up from wherever the hell she's whoring

around and tell her I haven't killed myself. I'm telling you that too, in case you're interested.

— You haven't killed yourself.

— Exactly, go and tell her that, but run.

— I don't know if…

— The fact is I never really planned to do it. It was just a test, understand?

— A test.

— A test she certainly didn't pass. That whore. But I wouldn't give her the pleasure of …

— I don't know if now…

— Don't interrupt me! When I talk, you listen, cretin!

— Cre… what?

— You're not Miki, right? I haven't heard your voice for so long that…

— That's not my name…

— You've saved yourself, because if you were Miki, I'd go there right now and rip off your balls.

— Forget about my balls.

— Do you hear me?

— Right.

— I don't understand how you got there, you know? A woman as smart, as beautiful…

— Yeah, that's true. She is beautiful.

— Shut up!…a woman who could choose any man she wanted…

— She made the wrong choice, that's for sure.

— If that's an indirect…

— No, no, not at all.

— Right. Is that a saw I hear?

— An electric knife.

— Aha.

— I love her too, you know? We never spoke but…

— You never spoke?

— No, but I felt affection for her, just like that, suddenly…

— Do you mean you never spoke to her and you're…

— …I think it was because of the croissants…

— And you're there, you piece of shit, with her in the bathtub?

— Oh, it's not what you think, those were the orders of…

— You have no idea what I think, asshole! You're a piece of meat, that much is clear, a piece of meat made to fill the space I left.

— Don't think I don't have my…

— I bet you're one of those idiots from the gym, I always warned her about them.

— I go once in a while, yeah.

— How disgusting, she's fallen into the deepest part of the morass of decadence.

— Into what?

— Did you go to see a Meg Ryan movie?

— What?

— Answer me, cocksucker!

— No, no really, I'm telling you we never even spoke…

— I suppose you came directly to the point.

— That's…one way of putting it, yeah…

— Where did I go wrong?

— Oh, you shouldn't…

— What do you know about what I should do? She…she was like the oven that baked my bread, you know? Like… the field of cherry trees in my spring. And now, you. And it's finished.

— I understand. Though you may not believe it, this has hurt me as much as you. Don't blame yourself, please, maybe I'm the only one who's guilty.

— She was perfect.

— Oh, yeah.

— She would wake up, you know, like a kitten and all…

— Right. And the butter croissants.

— And the butter croissants…You know about the butter croissants?

— Well, that…

— That was ours, the croissants were our little game…oh, shit…

— Listen, don't get like…

— …sometimes with chocolate…

— Yeah, well…those, yeah…

— Maybe…maybe if I kill myself now…I don't have much left to live for…don't tell her, all right? Anyway…anyway… she won't care…In fact, neither will you…if committing suicide is a way to attract attention, it won't work for me at all…

— Take it easy, there's no need to add more tragedies to the ones that…

— …she won't care…

— Maybe…maybe you two should have talked before it was too late…

— Don't give me advice, dimwit.

— OK, OK, but easy, yeah? There's lots of women…

— Yeah…I guess so.

— You go to the market and meet some, you meet others at the movies and like that, and, I don't know, in your life, through friends…

— I don't have any friends…

— Man, you don't need to be melodramatic…

— I keep hearing that thing…

— I'm finished, never mind.

— Well, I guess that…

— That's it, you won't hear it any more…

— You're not such a bad guy, you know?

— Thanks.

— Don't let the things I said bother you, OK? It was…passion…you know.

— No problem.

— I suppose Esmeralda knows why she makes the decisions…

— Who?

— What do you mean who? Didn't you even ask her name?

— Her name isn't…

— Esmeralda, yes sir, and I'm telling you I've slept with her in that same bed many more times than you.

— That's a pretty name.

— Sure it is.

— But it's a mistake.

— Ah?

— I saw that name on the mailbox downstairs, but she lives next door. It's strange, isn't it? To mix up telephone numbers and addresses. There's an Esmeralda on this floor, but in apartment B.

— Yeah, exactly. Right where you are. Six B…It's funny you haven't…Hello? Hello? Are you there?

— …

— Are you there or what? What damn manners.

— That's right, it's B. Shit.

— Are you all right? You've become like…I don't know…I was the one who was angry, remember. "You pile of shit" and all that…

— Right. Yeah. Shit.

Click.

— Hey, listen. Are you there? Is everything all right? Did you hang up?

(415) 952–3144

4:24 A.M.

— Hello?

— I think I behaved very badly the last time we talked…I… didn't mean to shout at you, and it isn't true that I think our relationship isn't going to work…and you don't have to leave your job or anything like that, you know? It's just that I became confused and…I'm like that sometimes, impulsive… but I love you, more than anything I love you and I don't care what you do or what you say, the only thing I know is that without you I'm nothing and it isn't even worth leaving this hole of an office to try to go to the bathroom, simply nothing…is worth it. Please forgive me, and don't leave me, and don't let me leave you, and let's give ourselves another chance. Yeah, that's it, let's give ourselves another chance…I think… I think we can be very happy together, I mean, we don't even have to see each other or anything, right? It's enough for me to hear you. Your voice is…your voice is like a green traffic light for me, like an alarm clock…or something like that. Do you forgive me, Conchita?

— Conchita doesn't work here any more, handsome. But I

can give you another chance.

— She doesn't…

— Ohhhh. You have a real man's voice.

— What do you mean she doesn't…

— Where are you?

— Not that…What do you mean Conchita doesn't…

— I don't know. She left this morning.

— But, is she all right? Did something happen to her? Do you know where to find her?

— I think she went to work in a chicken store or something like that.

— Chicken.

— Maybe fish.

— Right.

— I don't remember.

— And where could…

— I'm sorry. The girls don't leave their numbers when they leave here. They prefer it that way.

— They prefer it…

— It's better.

— Sure.

— Do you want a blow job? An erotic dance? Necrophilia? Zoophilia? Paralyzed?

— I want…Oh, God…

— I don't know that position. But if you describe it…

— Oh no. It's just that…You don't understand.

— Don't underestimate me, baby.

— Sure, I'm sorry.

— I want your come in my mouth.

— Seriously?

— Oh, yeah, you're so big. And it's so thick.

— What should I say.

— You're not cooperating.

— Oh, sorry. It's just that…I was hoping to find…

— Yeah, I got that.

— Are you offended?

— …

— Did I offend you? Ohh, I'm sorry. That wasn't…that wasn't my intention…

— I can eat your balls like chocolate bonbons, you hear me?

— Sure…

— …And jerk you off until you don't even have any snot left…

— I'm sure you can…You don't have to…don't get so…

— A couple of days ago, an old man called me and I gave him a heart attack…

— Seriously?

— And I wasn't even trying very hard. Just the normal thing. Besides, he fell down and left the phone off the hook. The call lasted like three and a half hours before somebody noticed and hung up.

— You did very well…

— My boss congratulated me and all. And then along comes an idiot who doesn't want to let me show…

— Don't blame me, please…

— Show my talent for this…

— It isn't…

— Everybody says I have a talent for this!

— I'm really sorry. It's just that…I'm dying. Can you understand that?

— You're…

— I'm dying, yeah.

— Then you're much worse off than me.

— And sometimes I say stupid things.

— You sure do.

— Will you forgive me?

— Well, I don't know, it doesn't matter. As long as you keep
talking…

— What?

— It's your money, you know? As long as you keep talking,
it's all the same to me.

— Really?

— Aha.

— Can I talk about what I…about whatever I want?

— I guess so.

— Love?

— Mmmmh. All right.

— I loved Conchita.

— Right.

— I mean…Haven't you ever fallen in love?

— Yeah, I guess so. With a drunk truck driver. He took my
money and in exchange he left me four kids and a case of
herpes, and took off with the first bitch he met on a run to
the coast.

— But…when you were with him, did you like him?

— I guess so. He was better than our schnauzer. At least he
didn't have distemper.

— You see? That's love.

— …Though sometimes he came home drunk and I had to tie him to the bed so he wouldn't beat up the neighbors and all. Señora Quequini was getting fed up with him…

— Señora Quequini.

— …But then she fell into a coma and forgot about him. Poor Señora Quequini.

— Poor thing.

— Wait, my boss is coming. I have to give you a fast blow job. All right?

— No problem.

— Bbbmmmff, sllrrrp, bbbuuurrrfff…

— Finished?

— Finished. It's just that a girl can't talk about just anything here.

— Ah, no?

— Oh, no. The boss wants us to work with professionalism.

— I understand…What's your name?

— Zelda, my name's Zelda.

— Zelda. Sounds nice.

— My real name's Vicky.

— Even better. Do you—do you have a coffee machine, Vicky?

— No. But we have a bubble gum dispenser.

— Brilliant. I have one for coffee.

— Coffee. Wow, I've always wanted a coffee machine, it's…

— You like coffee?

— It's the best. When I was little I would sneak all the coffee in the house.

— Seriously?

— I looked like an epileptic afterward.

— Ha! An epileptic!

— Yeah. I moved very fast. I gave it to my grandma too.

— Coffee to your grandma?

— Poor grandma. She died. One day she was in the garden, stuck out her tongue, and shit herself. That's dying.

— Horrible, isn't it?

— Oops. I'm sorry, I forgot you said you were…

— It's nothing. It's nothing.

— So you knew Conchita.

— Who? Ah, yeah…Briefly, we didn't get…

— No?

— We really didn't get into our friendship.

— Shame.

— Yeah. But with you…

— What?

— With you I feel…What did you say your name was?

— Zelda.

— Zelda. With you, Zelda, I feel we have a very special connection.

— Something special? Yeah?

— Sure.

— Then you can call me Vicky.

— Brilliant, Vicky.

— Brilliant.

— Yeah, brilliant.

(415) 937–0353

7:31 P.M.

— Welcome to our customer service center. If you need information about any of our products, press 1. To find out about bills and fees, press 2. If you…

2

— One moment please. We're here to serve you better. Taaaa-ta-ta-taaaa-ta-ta-ta-ta-ra-ra-raaaa-tiiii-ti-ti-tiiii-taa-ra-ra-ra-ra-ra-ta-ra-ra-taaaa-ta-ta-ta-raaaa-tu-ri-ru-taaaa-ta-ta-taaaa-ta-ta-ta-ra-ra-raaaa-tiiii-ti-ti-tiiii-taa-ra-ra-ra-ra-ta-ra-ra-taaaa-ta-ta-ta-raaaa-ru-ri-ru-taaaa-ta-ta-taaaa-ta-ta-ta-ta-ra-ra-raaaa-tiiii-ti-ti-tiiii-taa-ra-ra-ra-ra-ra-ra-ra-taaaa-ta-ta-ta-raaaa-tu-ri-ru-taaaa-ta-ta-ta-aaa-ta-ta-ta-ta-ra-ra-raaaa-tiiii-ti-ti-tiiii-taa-ra-ra-ra-ra-ra-ta-ra-ra-taaaa-ta-ta-ta-raaaa-tu-ri-ru This is Remi. How may I help you?

— I'd like to speak to the sales representative Jorge, please.

— One moment, please. We're here to serve you better. Taaaa-ta-ta-taaaa-ta-ta-ta-ta-ra-ra-raaaa-tiiii-ti-ti-tiiii-taa-ra-ra-ra-ra-ra-ta-ra-ra-taaaa-ta-ta-ta-raaaa-tu-ri-ru-taaaa-ta-ta-taaaa-ta-ta-ta-ta-ra-ra-raaaa-tiiii-ti-ti-

tiiii-taa-ra-ra-ra-ra-ra-ta-ra-ra-taaaa-ta-ta-ta-raaaa-tu-
ri-ru-taaaa-ta-ta-taaaa-ta-ta-ta-ta-ra-ra-raaaa-tiiiii-ti
ti-tiiii-taa-ra-ra-ra-ra-ra-ta-ra-ra-taaaa-ta-ta-ta-raaaa-tu-
ri-ru-taaaa-ta-ta-taaaa-taa-ra-ra-ra-ra-ra-ta-ra-ra-taaaa-
ta-ta-ta-raaaa-tu-ri-ru-taaaa-ta-ta-taaaa-ta-ta-ta-ta-ra-ra-
raaaa-tiiiiii-ti-ti-tiiii-taa-ra-ra-ra-ra-ra-ra-ra-taaaa-ta-
ta-ta-raaaa-tu-ri-ru- This is Jorge. How may I help you?

— This is Godínez. X-3459362-Y.

— How may I help you, Señor Godínez?

— I don't know.

— Let me look it up in the file…aaah…Reginaldo Godínez,
correct? You have a transaction open for doub…

— Forget about that, Jorge.

— What?

— You know? We haven't always treated each other well
and…

— Excuse me, sir, do we know each other?

— Yes, damn it, of course we know each other, we talk on
the phone every day. You're the only fucking person I talk to
every day. Don't say you don't know me because…

— I'm sorry, sir. I'm here to serve you.

— I just…wanted…to talk to you because…I don't know…
from one moment to the next, you know?

— Yeah…

— From one moment to the next, I thought… it can all
end…understand me?

— Do you mean…the billing? The line? One of our special
services?

— Everything, Jorge. I don't know whether…I don't know

whether you're aware…

— Oh, that would be terrible, sir.

— Right. That's why I was thinking, you know? That maybe… if…well…it all ended, it would make no sense to keep feeling hatred or resentment toward you…

— Hatred?

— But really! Are you talking or am I?

— You are, sir.

— The fact is I thought all—all about love and death, I don't know if you understand…

— …Yes, sir?

— Well, and it occurred to me…that we're very small and… don't talk much to each other…Don't you think so? Or we talk to each other but it's as if…as if we weren't really talking and…

— We have a three-way conference service, sir. And in our program 5 you can call five more people…

— Right, but it isn't enough.

— Do you wish us to keep you informed about future offers and promotions?

— I don't think that…I don't think any of that is enough.

— Perhaps if you tell me your needs, I…

— I need…I need a new job, or at least not to be fond of my job…I need someone to bring me croissants in the morning…

— Butter or chocolate?

— …I guess either one would be fine…I'm…

— The chocolate are my favorite…

— …I'm not very demanding, you know?

— I'm sorry, sir. We only have telephones.

— Telephones.

— Yes.

— Well, I guess I can't ask for croissants where there are telephones, right?

— I guess not, sir.

— In any case…

— You can also request special services.

— In any case it's been nice talking to you, Jorge. I feel better.

— Thank you, sir.

— It isn't always easy to find an attentive ear, right?

— It's easier to buy a new phone.

— Sure. Sure it is.

— You can't ask very much of them, but there are some very nice models.

— Right. Thank you, Jorge.

— We're here to serve you, sir.

(415) 237–3014

11:30 AM

— Hello, this is Mary. If you're hearing this message, it means I'm not in, OK?…

— Shit, Reginaldo. Shit, shit, shit.

— …But give me your number, and if I have time…

Click

— Hello?

— M…Mary?

— Is that you, Don, you rotten son of a bitch?…

— M…Mary, my love…

— Last night I had to take three Lexotan. I was waiting for you with wine and candles like an imbecile!

— Yeah, well…

— And you're still not here!

— Yeah… it's just that…

— Let me talk to your wife, asshole! Let's settle this once and for all!

— Oh, Mary…I…I'm sorry…you have to understand…

— You said that…

— My wife had… a…fainting spell, yeah…it wasn't the right time, you know? A sensitive man can't…

— I can! I want to talk to her.

— Oh, no…cream cake…not now…

— You promised, Don! You're playing with my feelings!

— Next weekend…I swear to you that next weekend I…

— You said the same thing on Wednesday!

— Right, but…you know…a fainting spell…

— And I had three Lexotan…

— I promise you that this time…

— It's a lie!

— But my love, just give me a few days…

— Will you, Don? Will you really?

— Oh, sure I will Mary…Sure I will.

— It's just that I don't know whether…

— Please. Please. Don't make me beg.

— Friday.

— Friday.

— You're not lying to me?

— Oh, Mary, you offend me. Do you think I could lie to you? There are things that …

— No, it's all right…

— There are things that really…

— Oh, Don, it's just that…

— You don't have to cry, Mary…

— It's just that I need you so much…

— It's all set, just…have a little patience…

— Friday.

— Friday, I swear.

— Oh, Don…

— Oh, Mary…

(415) 496–6642

4:44 P.M

— You've reached Palomares 5, Six B. No representative is in the house at the moment. Leave your name and number and we'll return your call. If you wish to make an offer to purchase the house, call Indeisa Real Estate Services at 214449966. Thank you.

— Hello, Esmeralda. I...well, I know you don't live there anymore...But...this is still your number and this is your house, so I didn't know where else to call you...Do you remember when I said nobody knows where to call a dead person? Well now I've confirmed it...umm...excuse me, I didn't mean to call you dead...though you are dead, I mean, it's a question of manners, right? If you see a paralyzed girl on the street, you don't say "Paralyzed girl! Paralyzed girl!" do you? Well, I just...just wanted...to tell you I spoke to your boyfriend...yeah...a little while before... I liked him, to tell you the truth, he seemed like a good guy. It's a shame he didn't defend you...you know? I'm not making comparisons, but I would've been there to die before you, or at least I wouldn't have allowed your dead body to be cut into pieces, you know? I mean, I would've said "Please, not in pieces" because it shows a lack of respect and all for the dead…oh, forgive me, I've said it again…but it's just that I don't know what to call you: The cadaver? The deceased? The expired?… Whatever it is, it's given you enough to deal with, cutting you into pieces is going a little too far, I don't know. It's funny that I spoke to you…about committing suicide and all… and now the dead one is you, I mean, I don't mean it's funny, it's more like…strange, isn't it? Well, whatever, the guy who was in your house…he wasn't a bad guy, you know? Though he didn't have the courage to defend you. What struck me was that you didn't get to know each other better, I mean, Esmeralda, you have the right to be a whore, you have all the right in the world, you know? but it's kind of…kind of ugly that…you come and…with a man who…I mean you didn't even see a Meg Ryan movie together, Esmeralda, really, you ought to be grateful a decent guy found you, I'm saying that because, I don't know, it's a risk, you know? To bring just anybody into your bed or into your bathtub—he told me you were in the tub…I think it's pretty whorish on your part and very bad taste to lounge in the bathtub with that bastard while I'm talking to him on the phone, but now it doesn't matter any more because you're dead, and the dead are forgiven everything, how whorish they are and all…forgive me, I called you dead again…I've been trying to find a movie on the adult channel with dead people, you know? One called "Necrophobia" or something like that maybe, but I haven't found anything, it seems it isn't normal, so I think our affair is over, Esmeralda. Well. After what happened the police came, you know? First you were on the news and then police came. They didn't want pizza or beer and they took me to the station and asked me very strange questions, Esmeralda, about you and me…I think I'm also calling you to beg your pardon, Esmeralda, because I told them horrible things. I told them I hated Meg Ryan, yeah. But it's true, I hate her! And that I didn't want…well…I didn't want, you know? I didn't want you to leave me…I said that, I didn't want you to go, because since then I've been like, I don't know, strange, you know? Umm, I feel strange. Different. I also told them you were a whore, I said that. At first they showed a lot of interest and were very friendly, but then they became peculiar, Esmeralda, and I swear I didn't understand anything. They asked me why I cut you into pieces, and I must admit that…well, that I had thought about cutting you into pieces at some point and all…but I didn't cut you into pieces. I would have poisoned you, or left you in a garage with the exhaust…well, if I had a car and a garage…but cutting into pieces isn't my style. You know? Or I would have hung you from the balcony but, of course, you never would've let me use the balcony, I know, because you're egotistical, I mean, I already talked to you about that…and if I had cut you into pieces, I wouldn't have left you scattered all around the house, you know? No way. Maybe I would've put you in a suitcase and thrown you in the river, I mean, I don't know, but I don't think I could've let you die alone. It's just that… ever since I heard what happened to you I want…I want to die too, you know? Because now I don't know where to call you, I mean, I'm calling you here but don't think you'll get back to me, and not because you're with your coffee and newspaper but because...well because you're not, right? I don't know if you understand me...Before you didn't return my calls, but you could...and I knew that at some point you'd hear my messages and you...and you'd do it and we'd talk and I'd run to your house with my fly already open—not *still* open—and we'd be together forever, it was only a question of time, but now there's no more time for us, right? I mean, if you got back to me and left me a message I wouldn't know where to find you to go to the movies and sit in the sixth row center and once in a while, only once in a while, read subtitles to you because you refused to wear your glasses, Esmeralda. Who reads subtitles to you now? And who am I talking to now? Who am I calling "whore" with all the affection I use when I say it to you? You'll say I still have Miki and Angela, sure, but the police said they didn't want to see me and they gave the cops tapes of... of calls I made to them and that they had processed. The words that came out of my mouth. Isn't it incredible? Words, and I didn't know whose ears they'd end up in, they even put them on television and wow! I feel like a star, but I'm afraid...I mean...I don't want to be a star without you, you know? I don't want to be anything without you...I explained it to the cops and they were nice...nice like the guy who was in your house that night...they said they'd take me to...and I'd be fine, right? A quiet place to rest my bones...yeah...I guess you have the advantage because you can rest your bones in several places at the same time...heh...excuse me...just a joke...I know, I shouldn't...I know...Do you remember when we made jokes together, Esmeralda? Do you remember when we did everything together? I liked it so much…Well, I don't want to bother you, and it's better if I don't keep talking, because if I keep on I'll say things… Besides, they only let me make one call and the time is running out. I only wanted to say that…I mean…wherever you are…I love you and will call you when I can, OK? So you won't feel alone or…and if I run into your friend, the one from that night, I won't kill him or anything because you have the right to…I mean…and everything I said to you before about your being a whore and all isn't true…I said it because…well, because…because I love you… and it's a lie…it's a lie that you don't matter to me because really, Esmeralda, now that I'm here, I realize I don't miss the adult channel, or the pizzas, or the beers, or the people who go to the movies, or the meter and a half of sidewalk in front of my house, or the forty square meters of my apartment, or anything in the world, anything, zero, null set, that isn't you. And I don't care either whether my words reach anyone else, not even on TV, you know, if you're not…really. I promise…I promise to call you soon, Esmeralda, and if everything goes well, I'll catch up with you one of these days, however I can… and we'll be together again and watch the adult channel, by now I know the whole catalogue and there are some you'll love…Yeah…and we'll go see Meg Ryan too…

— …

— Oh, Esmeralda, "French Kiss" is awful, you have to choose another one…

— …

— No! Not that one either, you're taking advantage, you know? you're taking advantage of me…

— ...

— OK, maybe "When Harry Met Sally," it has that good scene of a faked orgasm, but don't insist too much, OK?... And afterward we'll walk the three hundred meters to my house and...

— ...

— Yeah! like a kitten...Yeah, I'll bring you breakfast...

— ...

— No, it's just...a speck got into my eye...It's all right now, see?...

— ...

— It's nothing. You...you keep talking, talk to me...Oh, Esmeralda, it's so wonderful to hear you again...

DESPOILER

At the age of thirty-nine, Carmen had resigned herself to being alone. She wasn't pretty, wasn't ugly either, and that ordinariness translated to all the areas of her existence: not rich and not poor, not stupid and not exceptional. Her characteristics were so normal—so indistinct—that Carmen attributed her lack of companionship to an overly demanding temperament, or, as a last resort, to luck. Not necessarily *bad* luck, simply the luck she had drawn.

It's not that she was an old maid or a prude. She'd had affairs in the course of her adult life. Some were pleasurable. Few were lasting. Most of her relationships had melted away over time, and those that survived the years tended to vanish when the moment came to make the definitive leap toward either matrimony or children. It wasn't—as her mother suspected—that men refused to marry her. It was often she who felt incapable of entering into a commitment longer than six or seven weekends. It was clear to her that she preferred to bear the burden of tedium alone rather than duplicate it. And if her sheets felt cold, a hot water bottle seemed a safer solution than a lukewarm partner.

Besides, to populate the world around her, her office colleagues were enough. Carmen worked near Calle Comercio, in a travel agency. Most of her work wasn't sending people out into the world but organizing the tourists—increasingly numerous—who visited Barcelona. So in a sense the agency wasn't a point of departure but a journey's end, a final destination, something that its physical location stressed: lost among the winding alleys of the Born district, squeezed into a blind alley beneath a vaguely ancient arch, practically invisible to pedestrians, the office resembled a bewitched cave in a forest.

The advantage of this situation was that clients didn't normally come to the agency, which encouraged a certain intimacy among the staff members. Among Carmen's four colleagues—Dani, Milena, Lucía, and Jaime—a camaraderie had been established, warm but respectful of personal lives, which allowed them to share joys without invading anyone's privacy. So when Milena's mother died, everyone attended the funeral to be with her. And when Jaime had pneumonia, the others took turns bringing him consommés at home. But when cysts were discovered that affected Carmen's renal function, she didn't want to bother anyone with her medical problem. And when her last boyfriend dropped her—Carmen remembered it well because this one actually did hurt her when he left—she spent days shut in the bathroom crying but never told her colleagues about her pain. She didn't even tell Daniel, the homosexual, with whom she shared more confidences. Carmen knew she could count on his support in little things but feared that if she asked for or needed more, she would cross the line that separates comradeship from emotional blackmail.

The agency's private calendar was marked by celebrations, the most important of which were birthdays. Five times a year, after the agency closed, the group celebrated the birthday of one of its members. They usually collected money from everyone to give the celebrant a significant present, almost always perfume. And they blew out the candles on a cake, though since the girls were always on a diet, chocolate cake eventually was reduced to a muffin and coffee. These ceremonies included the repetition of the same jokes each time, and even though they weren't an orgy of diversion, Carmen liked them: she enjoyed the security of small quotidian rituals that made her life a place without surprises, easy to manage.

Even so, the day she turned forty, the plan was more daring than she expected. The date coincided with Carnival, and someone in the office—perhaps Lucía, who was slightly excessive—had suggested that they all put on costumes and go from bar to bar. Carmen thought Carnival in Barcelona was picturesque, and one year she had watched it, but only as a witness, as herself, feeling protected in her normalcy while around her teemed the most extravagant simian masks. She was prepared to do it again on those terms, placing a prophylactic distance between herself and Carnival, smiling at the most ingenious costumes as one smiles at a show on stage. The problem, to her horror, was that the office staff had announced a *surprise*, which undoubtedly would include an obligatory costume.

Carmen hated all those things: surprises, costumes, and what she called "unruliness in the street." She thought they were childish entertainments absolutely inappropriate for responsible adults. But refusing would have meant introducing an element of confrontation into her healthy workplace coexistence, and she was not prepared to put her small universe at risk. Besides, there really was no Plan B for the night. If she rejected this one, she would have to eat supper with her mother. And she would expose herself to anything, even going out dressed as a monster, to avoid having to eat supper with her mother on the night of her birthday.

For as long as Carmen could remember, her mother had ruined all her birthdays. She was an extroverted woman who loved parties and guests and always had the house filled with people. As a consequence, she tried to turn her little girl's birthday into a great children's social event. She moved all the furniture out of the living room, bought tons of food and drinks, and handed out invitations right and left, even to girls who weren't her daughter's friends, or even worse, were her declared enemies. If Carmen protested, her mother explained that there was nothing like a party to make friends, and after all, no problem between girls her age could be that serious.

But Carmen—perhaps because of this—was a withdrawn, shy girl who slouched in a corner while her guests had a good time and her mother chatted with the adults. Often, as she tried to make herself invisible, she moved from hostess to victim of her guests. When the most hardened girls realized she would not react to any provocation, they thought up ways of torturing her: they pulled her braids. They pushed her. They laughed at her. They put gumdrops on her clothes. They stole her presents. And then, when her mother approached, they pretended everything was fine and obliged Carmen to smile and pretend, too. Of course, the first few times, Carmen tried to tell what was happening, but her mother responded:

"Honey, you have to learn to relax. Your friends are just playing."

And after these words, she obliged her to go play as well. She said she had to join in. Since the human world was hostile, Carmen took refuge in the world of her toys, especially her stuffed animals, which fascinated her. Her collection included a bear with button eyes, a zebra, a very plump cat, and a cow with fat, pink teats, among many others that hung from the walls and filled her closets. Carmen didn't treat these dolls as things but as friends. She would put them in a circle in the middle of her room and have a tea party. She allowed them to decide what they wanted to play. She slept with them, and when there were too many to fit under the sheets with her, she gave them her bed and slept on the rug on the floor. At least they deserved it, they deserved it more than people did.

Her favorite was a maroon wolf her father had brought her from Germany. She called it Max. When her mother asked where she got that name from, Carmen replied:

"That's what he wants to be called."

In fact, as if he had a life of his own, the wolf Max frequently showed up in the most unexpected places: in the knife drawer in the kitchen, under her parents' bed, in the bathtub. At the same time, Carmen showed up less and less. When she came home from school, she shut herself in her room with her animals and had to be pulled out for supper. If there were guests in the house, even if there were children, Carmen hid under her bed with all her animals. And more and more each day she seemed to communicate only with them, assigning Max the role of spy in the outside world.

If she had to communicate with adults, Carmen did so as a representative of the animals. She didn't ask for chocolate, she stated, "Max wants chocolates." If she didn't want to visit her grandmother, her excuse was that the bear or the cow was sick (the wolf was the only one with a name, but he never got sick). Even in her letters to The Three Kings, she asked only for things for her animals, the only creatures she seemed to think of as real. The one she wrote when she was nine said:

> Dear kings please bring a scarf for the bear who gets colds and a hat for my giraffe who's very tall and hits his head on the ceiling and for Max a girl wolf because he wants to have little wolves thank you.

That letter irritated her mother very much. For her, the worst punishment was isolation, and the girl was constructing hers with both hands. To combat this, she tried to take her on excursions to the Costa Brava, to the Olot volcano, to the thermal baths at Montbui. On these outings she included other children, as many as possible, until the family car was completely full. When they reached each site she let them out like a pack of animals so they could run on the grass and chase insects, in essence so they could let off steam and play. But as far as Carmen was concerned, it was useless. The girl behaved correctly, but with distant coldness. She obeyed instructions and took part in games without complaints or enthusiasm, as if this were a required but not difficult school assignment. And she did so with her head somewhere else, no doubt in her toy closet.

For birthday number ten, her mother decided to provoke some shock therapy. She organized the biggest of all the parties. She rented a games room and invited more than fifty people, quite an achievement considering her daughter's scant list of friends. She bought the girl a pink dress and instructed her for days to look sociable and be happy, willingly or by force.

On the day of the party, Carmen conferred all morning with her animals about what to do. She identified so thoroughly with them that their games were real assemblies, with debates and turns to speak. That morning, some of the stuffed animals suggested she get sick. Others, among them Max the wolf, supported direct insubordination: refuse to go.

But Carmen couldn't do that to her mother. For days she had seen her hurrying nervously from one preparation to another, and knew this party meant more to her than to the supposed celebrant. Besides, Carmen had developed the kind of shell that permitted her to function in the outside world in exchange for returning to her own safe and sound, and she didn't mind using it if necessary. In reality, it was the safest thing because it guaranteed that as long as she knew how to behave, nothing would change between her and her toys. And so, against the desires of her animals, she opted for the most diplomatic solution: she would attend the party and then return to her plush bubble to hibernate until her next birthday.

The most surprising thing is that she liked the party. Amused by the trampolines and the slides, the guests didn't torment her, and she could forget her fears and take part in the games. Aware of her fascination with them and unaware of her mother's concerns, some guests gave her stuffed animals: dogs, monkeys, hens, deer. But for once Carmen was more interested in people and was able to have a good time with them. That night, she returned home, her heart racing with the discovery of parties and her reconciliation with the world.

But when she tried to tell her animals all about it, they were no longer in her room.

Or in her closet.

Or under her bed.

Carmen searched the whole house. She emptied out drawers. She picked up rugs. She called for each of her animals, especially Max. Finally, fearing the answer she knew beforehand, she asked her mother what had happened to her friends. That's what she called them, *friends*, while tears rolled down her cheeks. And her mother's words fell heavily on her, like anvils hurled from heaven.

"You're too big for those things now, darling. It's time for you to find other pastimes."

The day she turned forty, Carmen opened her eyes ten minutes before the alarm clock rang and let the time drip slowly until it was time to get up. As she stripped in front of the mirror, she noticed the lines beginning to appear on her neck, under her arms, and between her breasts. She felt that her body came with an expiration date. She thought the custom of celebrating the passage of time with joy showed bad taste.

Throughout the day, her companions behaved with studied normality, which served only to make Carmen more nervous. From time to time she caught a glance of complicity among them, and she felt tempted to use a cold as a pretext and go home until the next day. In the afternoon, one of the clients wished her a happy birthday and winked at her. Carmen had the feeling the entire city knew, that she walked down the streets with a sign on her forehead that said: "Today I'm a day older."

After closing and doing the day's accounts, Jaime and Daniel turned off the light and emerged from the back with the traditional muffin that, thoughtfully, was Carmen's favorite: apple and cinnamon. It had two candles with the numbers 4 and 0 attached, which illuminated the scene faintly while her colleagues sang Happy Birthday. Carmen wanted everything to end there and blew out the candles. But she knew the muffin would not grant her wish.

Due to the proximity of the Easter Week vacation they were closing late, so they could simply change clothes and begin their "mad night," as Daniel called it in the gayest accent he could muster. And then the moment arrived that Carmen feared: with a *tadaaa* to make the occasion shine,

Milena and Lucía presented her costume, the material proof that no one could go back, that she would spend the night dressed as someone she wasn't, surrounded by faceless people.

The costume wasn't even original. Even worse, it was the most ordinary and trite of all: a prostitute. "A tart," as Daniel specified with a shriek. It had platform shoes and high colored stockings, a leather miniskirt with suspenders, and a black top, all of which left wide bands of flesh exposed. The good part was that at least on the street, she would have to wear her coat. The bad part was all the rest. Her companions weren't prodigies of creativity but undoubtedly had better costumes. Daniel wore the tunic and laurels of Caligula, and Jaime was a Goth, with a studded collar and leather and metal accessories. Milena was disguised as Little Red Riding Hood. Lucía was a policewoman. Each one went into the bathroom and came out to the applause and joking comments of the others. Carmen, who had been the first, was present at the spectacle, trying to maintain her composure but with the sensation that everything was happening a million light years away.

When they went out she confirmed with relief that they weren't the only ones around in costume. Vampires and astronauts paraded along the streets and tunnels of the neighborhood. In front of the wig shop on Calle Princesa, a goblin and a witch compared their false noses. Dogs and rats came up to the surface from the metro entrance on Plaza del Angel. For the first few minutes, the five office workers felt a nervous tingling because of the situation, which Daniel attempted to relieve with sexual jokes. But by the time they reached the Santa Caterina Market, they felt more comfortable in their new skins, which became confused with ceilings of multicolored mosaics and the surrealist atmosphere of the passersby. When they crossed Vía Laietana, the long plush neck of a giraffe stood out against the profile of the buildings. And Carmen felt that, after all, her striptease attire was extremely conservative.

The esplanade of the cathedral confirmed that impression. Among unprepared tourists and pedestrians strolled gargoyles that seemed to have come down from the cornices. In single file so they could walk the narrow corridors of the Barrio Gótico, Carmen and her friends followed Daniel's tunic to a bar. When she went in, perhaps because of the nervousness she felt walking the streets dressed as she was, Carmen felt relieved, as if she had come to a place that was known, even welcoming.

The bar was decorated like a catacomb, and the air, filled with a dense smoke, gave the patrons the appearance of ghosts in the mist. Carmen ordered a double whiskey. She didn't normally drink, but she didn't normally face these situations either, and even though Lucía was playing games with her handcuffs and it all seemed amusing, she needed something to help her relax.

"The bad thing about Carnival," said Milena, "is that you can hook up with an ugly guy without realizing it. Since everybody's masked…"

"No," answered Jaime, "the good thing is that you can hook up even if you're ugly. It's a day of thanks for thousands of people…"

You had to shout to make yourself understood. And half the conversation didn't reach Carmen's ears, but she smiled anyway in order not to be left out. She wanted to go to the bathroom but would have to cross the human mass. She tried but couldn't get very far.

"Darling, he's looking at you," Daniel said in her ear.

At the bar, a wolf man had just ordered a drink. His body was covered with hair, and a shaggy tail moved back and forth.

"He didn't look at me," said Carmen.

"Sweetheart, believe me. I know when a man is looking at somebody. Even if it's not me."

Someone ordered another round of drinks, and one of them came to Carmen's hands. Her companions toasted and laughed, though Carmen wasn't sure why. The wolf man was closer to them now, and suddenly he was talking to Daniel. And soon afterward to all the others.

"You have a very good costume," said Carmen, just to say something. "You look like a real wolf."

"I *am* a real wolf," he replied.

And she laughed.

"Your costume is nice too. It's…exciting."

"I hate it."

Before she realized it, she had begun a conversation with the wolf man. At times, when she didn't hear what he said, she admired the perfection of his disguise. She didn't see zippers or seams, and the mask seemed to fit his face perfectly. After a while, Milena asked:

"Shall we go somewhere else?"

Almost automatically, they all began to push toward the exit. When she reached the door, Carmen noticed a bear in a scarf drinking at the back of the bar. She had the impression that his eyes were like two buttons.

When she was out in the fresh air, Carmen discovered that she was slightly dizzy, and the wolf man—by then he had identified himself as Fran—offered her a hairy arm under her coat, and its touch seemed natural. They walked through a crowd of skeletons, lagging behind a little. When they turned a corner of arches and heavy bars, Carmen stumbled into a Che Guevara, who laughed out loud. In the square facing them was a metal camera watching her with its single eye. Carmen took some time to understand that it was a monument to something or someone.

"Where are we?" she asked her companion.

"It's along here."

They crossed a square surrounded by columns, with a fountain in the center, and palm trees. Carmen recognized the Plaza Real, but it seemed different from the way it usually looked. Perhaps it was the people leaning out the windows, who seemed to observe her in silence. As she left the Rambla, Carmen discovered she had definitively lost her friends.

"I'd swear they were right here," Fran assured her.

But then, and only then, Carmen guessed the true nature of her birthday *surprise*, a surprise that had Daniel's characteristic stamp and that, perhaps in the heat from the drinks, did not bother her: a hairy gift with large fangs named Fran:

"Do you want to go to another bar?"

Carmen noticed how tall Fran was. She saw him from

below, and his face was outlined against the full moon. He smiled. A woman disguised as a cow with large pink teats passed by, too drunk to walk without stumbling.

Darling, you have to learn to relax.

They crossed the Rambla into the Raval district. They passed a kind of ancient jail with thick bars at the windows. Carmen thought she heard a scream coming from the interior, but when she turned around, she saw only a man disguised as a cat, in a very fat costume. Fran didn't seem concerned. He had bought a beer from a Chinese man and offered her a sip. Carmen accepted. As they advanced, the crowd thinned out, and some streets were completely empty. Farther on, past the Rambla of Raval, Carmen began to discover that people weren't disguised as Moroccans. They were real Moroccans, and some of them whistled at her as she went by. The air smelled of kebabs and beer. On a corner, graffiti demanded: KILL THEM ALL.

Fran halted suddenly outside a place locked behind a metal gate.

"Fuck," he said, "I didn't think it would be closed today."

"I'm cold," Carmen protested, feeling the air filtering through her colored stockings.

Without saying anything, Fran led her to a narrow street that ran into an intricate network of passageways. They followed the labyrinth until they reached a building so narrow it had no room for an elevator. As they climbed the narrow staircase, Fran muttered something about his house and how he had drinks there. Carmen walked behind him, more because of cold than desire. She felt heavy and awkward, and wanted a sofa to lie down on. *And for Max a girl wolf because he wants to have little wolves thank you.*

Fran's house was surprisingly large considering how narrow the staircase was. It consisted of a single hall that circled a central courtyard and along which the rooms were distributed. The living room was only a widening of the hall, which seemed unending. Carmen curled up in an armchair and accepted the brandy her host offered. When she lifted the glass to her lips, she felt the drink, thick and hot, like Turkish coffee.

"Fran, can I call you Max?"

"You can call me anything you like."

A dry sound, like a blow, reached her from somewhere in the hall, but once again Fran didn't seem to have heard it. Carmen's feet were cold and she drank a little more. With each sip, Fran refilled her glass with that liquid that seemed less and less like brandy. The room spun around, and she had the impression there were more voices in it, though it was difficult for her to determine if they were outside or inside her head. Fran continued to wear his costume. The hair was so natural. It was like sitting next to a gigantic dog.

"Max, why don't you take off your mask? I haven't seen your face yet."

"Do you want me to take it off?"

Carmen nodded.

"Maybe you won't like what you see," he said, and she thought she detected a smile on his muzzle.

"Take it off." He raised his hands to the back of his neck. He moved his hands at the height of his neck and forced a little, as if the zipper was stuck. Carmen saw double, and her eyes struggled to close, but expectation held up her eyelids. At last, the wolf's face yielded. First it became slack in its contours, then definitively amorphous. Fran took it between his hands on both sides and pushed up. When the mask finally gave way, Carmen discovered the face that emerged beneath it. It was the face of her mother. And it was her voice that said, now with stentorian clarity, as if it were sounding from all the corners of the living room:

"You're too big now for those things, darling. It's time for you to find other pastimes."

In the next instant, Carmen saw only the open fangs approaching her face. And darkness.

Carmen opened her eyes ten minutes before the alarm clock rang and allowed the time to drip slowly until she had to get up. At first, it took her a few seconds to understand that she was in her house. Then, she tried to remember how she got back but couldn't. She attempted to think that in reality she hadn't gone out at night, but her costume—that awful costume—was thrown on the floor, like an uncomfortable witness. She got up and pushed it under the bed with her foot. She tried not to know that she had turned forty. That she'd ever had birthdays. The only reality, she told herself, is what happens in front of other people.

At least she could be sure that at work no one would ask. She had that kind of relationship with her colleagues, one that was respectful of privacy. She absolutely could decree she had never had a party with apple and cinnamon muffins.

Perhaps even if she asked, the others wouldn't remember either. Perhaps the previous day hadn't even registered, and they were waiting for her with mischievous smiles and a tart's costume, ready to celebrate Carnival.

When she stripped in front of the mirror, she noticed the lines that were beginning to appear on her neck, under her arms, between her breasts. She felt that her body came with an expiration date. She thought the custom of celebrating the passage of time with joy showed bad taste.

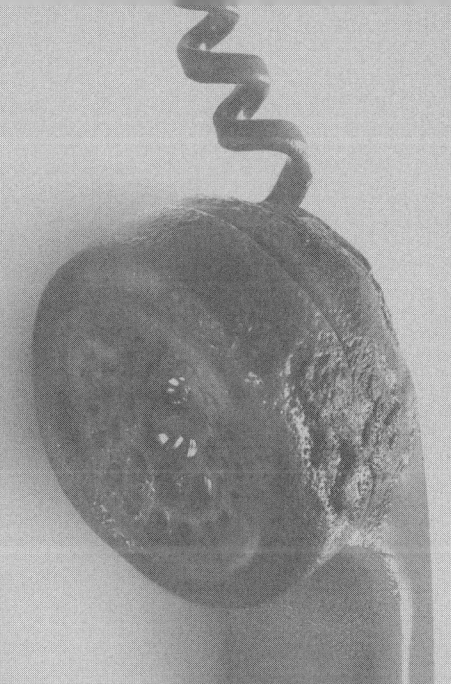

BUTTERFLIES FASTENED
WITH PINS

One gets used to anything. I'm getting used to my friends committing suicide.

First it was Fats Reboiras, with his round face of a sixty-kilo baby. Fats was my companion in not playing soccer at school. We spent recreation periods sitting together on the field watching everybody else play. Sometimes we ducked to avoid being hit by the balls that got away from the game. Fats always got the worst of it because he was a bigger target. We never talked very much.

Once, when we were leaving school, Fats invited me to his house to see his butterfly collection. They were dead butterflies, fastened with pins to a black cloth in a box of wood and glass. He had a lot of them, from enormous moths to small blue tropical ones. His father collected larger animals because he was a hunter. In the living room there were heads of bears, elk, and even a tiger, but he had bought the tiger, as Fats admitted. He kept long weapons in a showcase. Rifles and things like that. That afternoon we played Pac-Man and had cookies and milk. Then he let me look at his sister sunbathing by the pool. He told me his sister was very hot and he'd let me see her for free. He was a good guy, Fats. I wanted to tell him I'd had a good time at his house, but we never did talk very much.

One Friday, I brought a Masters of the Universe comic to school so he could see how much he looked like Ram Man. They were identical. But Fats didn't come to school that day. The following Monday, after singing the school song and the Peruvian anthem, a priest announced to the entire school that Fats had died accidentally. He asked us to pray but I didn't pray, because Fats Reboiras was sure to go to hell for showing me his sister.

When I asked the priest what had happened, he told me that Fats had suffered an accident cleaning one of his father's weapons. When I heard that it seemed believable, but now I wonder why Señor Reboiras had sent his eleven-year-old son to clean his hunting rifles. I think Fats just killed himself, though maybe he hadn't planned to. Those things happen.

A few years later I became friends with Julián. We were fifteen but he had lived as if he were forty. His drug problems obliged him to repeat the second year of secondary school. In the third he was expelled for insulting the headmaster's mother. That was good for us. Since he was no longer a student, he could stop by and visit us with bottles of pisco and rum that we drank in secret during recreation periods, hiding behind the biology lab.

When we reached fourth year, Julián was completely intoxicated and tried to sell marijuana to ten-year-olds at the entrance to the school. He managed to stay out of the reformatory, but that cost his parents all the money they had saved for a cottage on the beach. They spent it just on bribing officials. In addition to that, they intended to place Julián in Eternal Peace, a detox facility where, it was learned years later, the patients were abused. In one case, the director raped one of the minor residents. This wasn't known when my friend's parents were thinking about putting him there. Fortunately (and just in time), Julián fell in love with Mili, and reformed almost immediately.

Mili had freckles, light eyes, and an apple-pie face. She wasn't as hot as Fats Reboiras's sister, but she was cute. And she saved Julián's life. After he began going out with her, he didn't buy any more marijuana or coke or anything. He began to play sports and walk Mili home at night. It must have been nice. Mili and Julián, reforming. After dating for two years, Mili left Julián. It seems she took up with Luchito Cárdenas, who was an asshole. The same day she left him, Julián called Shorty Cabieses (or was it Blacky Espichán?) and told him he loved him, bro, and would miss him. Shorty (or Blacky) didn't understand anything but was worried.

He ran to Julián's house and rang the bell. Julián's mother opened the door. From upstairs you could hear Iron Maiden playing at top volume in his room. His mother asked Shorty to tell Julián to turn down the music. Shorty ran up the stairs and tried to go in the bedroom, but the door was locked. He knocked and shouted and called. Julián didn't answer. Shorty went downstairs to tell Julián's mother to open the door. She looked for the bedroom key in a drawer in her bedroom. She didn't find it. She called her husband. He shouted that she couldn't control Julián, that it was all her fault, that she had raised her son very badly.

During all this time, Shorty kept knocking on our friend's door. When the shot was fired, he wanted it to be an Iron Maiden drum.

At the wake Julián wore a hat to hide the hole in his head. His mother cried more than his father, but I think that's normal. On the day of the burial, Blacky Espichán wanted to be the first to arrive. He became so annoying that I told him, "Take it easy, Blacky, Julián isn't going anywhere." But he didn't laugh.

The following year I went to the university. I must have spent the entire first year very drunk, because I remember very little. It was 1992, a coup took place, and there was a bar across from the university. Leo's. I had lots of friends and they were all in Leo's. Drool was there. Drool had graduated school with me but hadn't been able to put it behind him. He was one of those people who remembered "the good old days" of a year ago with nostalgia, cried at having left the school, and sang the school song when he was drunk, and when he was sober too (but he was always pretty drunk). For getting into the university, he had been given a car.

I don't know if I ought to include Drool on the list, because he didn't commit suicide like the others. Though maybe he did. He always drove so fast—and so drunk—that we all knew something would happen to him one day. Until it happened: he crashed into a tree at the edge of the Olivar de San Isidro. With him were Kiki Frisancho—who broke an arm—and Mario and Jimena, who suffered only minor bruises. The only one who came out of the accident in a coma was Drool.

His friends spent several days at the hospital entrance, waiting for news and trying to do something when there was nothing to do. We were so bored we sneaked up to his room to see him connected to the respirators and then came down to tell the others about it. On the fifth day, his father managed to come back from England, where he lived, to order the machines turned off. Drool couldn't be connected indefinitely. We all understood.

They buried Drool in a black suit that was too big for him, and with a ball of cotton in his mouth, its threads sticking out between his lips. He had on a silk tie that must have been his father's.

I didn't tell any jokes that day.

After what happened to Drool, we all stopped drinking for something like two days. Then everything went back to normal. The rest of my classes in arts and letters were monotonous but fun. When I finished the general classes, I began to study linguistics. I wanted to study literature, but the people in literature were always saying incomprehensible things about strange books. At least I had never heard the people in linguistics, because there were very few of them.

Soon after I enrolled I met Javier Tanaka. Tanaka was an expert in Don Quixote. He knew all the editions perfectly and rolled his own cigarettes very calmly, with a huge smile. He was fun and unmistakably a dwarf.

One day my throat became inflamed. And remained inflamed for more than two weeks. I went to the doctor. In the public hospital there was an ear-nose-and-throat special-ist named Tanaka. I chose him. He was an austere, silent man who did his work and barely spoke to me. At one point I asked him if he was Javier's father. Yes, he said. He said nothing else. I remarked that I studied with his son. Right, he replied. He prescribed an injection in the ass that they gave me at the nearby pharmacy where the sanitary conditions were lamentable, but they didn't charge much. Some days later, I remarked to Tanaka that I had met his father. Tanaka said: "ah."

I thought they weren't on speaking terms, but I found out they lived together. Maybe that's why they weren't on speaking terms.

Two days after receiving a scholarship to an exchange program in Spain, Tanaka died. The maid found him lying face-up on his bed. The sheets were covered with froth from his mouth. His family denied it was a suicide. They called it an accident. According to what Skinny Céspedes told me, Tanaka took more pills than at a rave on Ibiza. But they weren't hallucinogens or anything like that. Tanaka needed amphetamines to wake up and barbiturates to sleep. Maybe he really didn't commit suicide. Maybe he simply took more than his usual amount or mixed it with alcohol from the celebration of the trip to Spain he would never take now.

Or maybe it was just the opposite, and he had tried to die for years until one day, by accident, he succeeded. He had been sad for several days and loneliness hung around his neck. One day before he died, he invited my friend Rony to have a cup of coffee. He wanted to talk to him. Rony broke the date because he had to turn in a paper on medieval literature. He said he'd see him the next day. Rony will always feel bad about not meeting Javier. He says that since then, when he drinks a cup of coffee, it seems to him he's drinking the foam on Tanaka's sheets.

About this time, another of my friends was sending strange signals from the planet of the dead. His name was Alex Antúnez and he was a poet, a bad thing. Poets from Peru always kill themselves. Luis Hernández threw himself in front of a train, Vallejo let himself die in life, Moro, a homosexual, went to work in a military academy, Adán committed himself voluntarily to an insane asylum, Heraud organized a band of guerrillas but was the only one killed because everyone else ran away when they saw his corpse. Alex Antúnez didn't want to be the exception.

Alex had been at my school too (a lot of people from my school were declared dead) before his frustrated attempt to enter a Jesuit seminary and a brief effort to dedicate himself exclusively and entirely to poetry, an effort that lasted three days.

After that he went to the university, where I met him because we taught quiz sections in the same group. The first time we went to give a class, we had a beer together to calm our nerves. I liked Alex. Months later, we organized a party to collect funds for a literary magazine. When we had all had too much to drink, Alex tried to kiss me. I told him I respected him but liked women, and I really felt like an imbecile.

Our relationship cooled a little, but we continued to talk when we ran into each other at the university. Alex would say that he wanted to start psychological treatment but had no money. He told me this when he punched a cop in the face and spent the night at the police station, when he went to bed with one of his students, and when he pulled down his trousers in front of the dean of the law school. After that I lost track of him.

As time passed, I heard that he had gone into the jungle, had finally published his book of poems, and had married. His marriage surprised me, but more than anything what surprised me was the news that he had a daughter. The last few times I saw him we barely said hello. He was wearing beads from the jungle and seemed happy.

I was already in Spain when I had an e-mail telling me about the fire in his house. His wife had discovered it when she returned from shopping. Smoke was pouring out of the windows. She tried to open the door but it was locked from the inside. She called the fire department. When they knocked down the door, they found Alex, or what remained of him, clasping a copy of his book open to the last page, and the lines that said:

I want to belong to air
That's why I burn my body

I don't know whether Alex was a coward or a brave man. I ask myself the same question about all the others. But in all my rosary of friends who were suicides—solitary, maladjusted, and lifeless—the one who intrigues me most is the one woman. The gorgeous Bel Murakami (apparently, the

Japanese are enthusiastic about suicide. They even consider it an honorable exit).

What happened with Bel was different. She wasn't my friend.

I only had an incredible desire to fuck her.

Bel was a legend among the heads of quiz sections. One of my colleagues, Andrés Molina, dedicated himself to developing a ranking of the most desirable female students and modifying it according to the suggestions of other members of the teaching team. He would spend hours in the rotunda of the school of letters "weighing the merchandise," that is, fantasizing and telling smutty jokes about each year's new aspirant to the throne of the "golden babe." When Bel Murakami arrived, Molina immediately declared her the "babe of the millennium" and never again made lists of successes. I would sometimes see her during this time, and I voted for her too but never met her personally.

Years later, shortly before I left Peru, I saw her in the audience of a concert where one of my stepbrothers was singing. Bel looked sensational. But that night I was with my friend Daniela. Though Daniela was just my friend, it seemed impolite to leave her hanging to talk to another girl. Besides, I've never had the least idea of how you talk to a girl you don't know in order to take her to bed. It's a technique that all my friends—alive and dead—seem to have down pat. But I've never mastered it.

In the middle of the concert, the girl at the table behind us had an epileptic seizure. People were frightened, the concert stopped, and my friend Daniela hurried to help the sick girl because Daniela wants to save the world. Suddenly I found myself beside Bel Murakami, without uncomfortable companions and with a perfect topic of conversation. We talked about epilepsy. About what you had to do, what brings it on, what risks it entails. She said that in the middle of a seizure it's a good idea to put a spoon in the victims' mouth so they don't bite their tongues and mutilate themselves.

The seizure ended and everything calmed down faster than I expected. Daniela returned to my table and Bel to hers. She seemed to be alone.

I didn't manage to ask for her number, but the next time I saw my stepbrother I told him that at his concert I'd met a very attractive girl. I mentioned Bel's name. My stepbrother was horrified. He said he'd been her boyfriend and that she was crazy. Crazy, crazy, crazy, he repeated. Hysterical. He told me she'd gone to the concert just to fuck with him, to fuck with his new girlfriend in particular who, in fact, had become furious.

In any event, on the nights that followed, each time I masturbated with the late-night porn stars, I gave them Bel's face.

I ran into her three days later in another bar. I was with my friends from the Kamasutra group—all of them drug addicts—and we had already been partying for hours. Fatal. When I saw her, I decided to go up to her, say something, ask for her phone number. I moved across the dance floor, through sweat and poking elbows. I raised my hand to greet her. She returned the greeting from the bottom of my glass. I kept moving. When I was only a couple of meters away,

I realized I was so drunk and so stupefied with coke that I'd embarrass myself in front of her. I couldn't even articulate words because my jaw was twitching. I was sweating. I wanted to vomit. When I saw that she was about to stand up, I smiled at her and continued on to the bathroom.

I saw her again only once in person and another time in effigy. The first time was months later, one night at a gas station where I stopped to buy beer. I was with a girl who wasn't even half as pretty as Bel, and she was with a guy who was a millionaire. We greeted each other with a movement of the head. I spent the rest of the night trying to forget I wasn't with her.

The last time I saw her she was in a Peruvian magazine that my father brought to me in Spain. There was a photo of Bel, who had just mounted a show of engravings. She was very thin, still beautiful, but she had at least fifteen kilos less beauty than in the week I'd fallen in love with her. My father knew her father. He said he thought he'd heard that the girl suffered from anorexia.

Two days ago, my friend Lorenzo wrote to tell me they had found Bel in the middle of the ravine across from the ocean in Lima. I imagine it was one of those days when the sky looks like a used carpet. Bel had thrown herself from the top but had only fallen—or rolled—about twenty meters. She's alive, but will stay in the hospital another two or three days because of various minor lesions. Lorenzo says he'd heard that Bel was pregnant—by somebody who isn't me— and that she lost the baby because of the fall. I hope it's only a rumor.

THE PASSENGER BESIDE YOU

It was only a scare.

Slamming on the brakes and the bang. Bangs. You're a little dazed but can move. You open the door and get out, not looking at the cab driver. Nothing hurts. You're a tourist. Your only obligation is to have a good time.

Lucky for you, a bus stops on the square. You get in and don't see where it's going. You walk to the back. Aside from the sleeping beggar, no one else is there. You sit down. You look out the window. The city and the morning spread out before your eyes. You take a deep breath. You relax.

At the first stop, a girl gets on. She's about twenty years old and very attractive. Blond. Everybody here is blond. She's the girl you've always wanted to sit beside you. She's dressed casually, in tight jeans and sneakers. Her coat is closed, but it suggests an overflowing white tee shirt. She sits beside you. You can't avoid looking at her.

You notice that she's looking at you.

At first it's imperceptible. But you notice it. She turns to look at you quickly out of the corner of her eye, for only an instant. When you return the look, she lowers her eyes again. She blushes. She tries to hide a smile. Finally, as if overcoming her shyness, she says flirtatiously:

"What are you looking at? Don't look at me!"

She looks away from you again, but now she can't help smiling. She makes a gesture, as if giving in to an impulse:

"Why are you looking at me so much? Huh? I know," and now she grows sad. "You can tell, right? You can tell? I thought you couldn't." She smiles mischievously. "Shall I show it to you? If you can tell, I don't have to hide it anymore. Do you want to see it?" She puts on an air of intrigue, assumes a complicit look, and speaks quietly, as if conveying a secret. "All right, take a look."

She opens her coat and reveals an enormous bullet wound in her heart. The rest of her chest is covered in blood.

She laughs roguishly, suddenly becomes serious, and announces:

"You see? I'm dead."

You don't notice it at first, right? You never notice it at first. I didn't even notice. It must be because it's the first time I've died. I'm not used to the change. One moment you're there and then the same old story: a stray bullet, a mugging, maybe a shoot-out between police and drug dealers, it happens every day. And then you're not there anymore. You know what I mean, right?

Besides, I was shot for being too sensitive. Really. For taking responsibility. Niki and I were going to a dog fight. Niki's my boyfriend and a war hero. Yeah. A war they fought not long ago…No. I don't remember where. Niki has a little dog named Buba and a pistol named Umarex CPSport. But he loves Buba more. He's a very professional dog. He's already torn three other dogs and a cat to pieces. He doesn't even leave their skins. Incredible. Niki loves him. He's his best friend, really. We were driving in the car then, and Niki and Buba were in front. I was in the back seat. Niki likes us to sit that way, he says it's the natural order of things. Niki's very orderly about his things. And very natural.

Leaving the city for the…Dog track? No, that's for races. What do you call the place where they fight dogs? Well, we were going there and stopped at a gas station so Niki could use the bathroom. Aside from a pistol and a dog, Niki has incontinence problems, but don't ever tell him that out loud, I mean it, for your own good. So Buba and I are alone in the car. Excuse the interruption, but don't look at my wound too much, please. I hate men who can't take their eyes off a girl's chest. And women too. If I weren't dead, I'd call Niki to make people respect me. OK? OK.

All right, we're in the car, right? Buba and me. And Buba begins to look at me with that face that means he wants to go to the bathroom. I mean, not to the bathroom, because he's an animal, right? But the closest thing to a bathroom that he can go to, OK? And he looks at me so I'll take him. Really, you wouldn't believe he's a killer dog if you saw the face he puts on when he wants to go to the bathroom. He drools from his cheeks, his eyes droop, and he makes these sweet little moans. So I look at him with his sad face, I understand him, you know? And I open the door so he can relieve himself.

Buba gets out and I go with him a few steps, but then I see that in the store in the gas station there's a sale on Revlon conditioners, so I stop because it's something important and he goes on. And then, another dog appears. I mean, a shit of a dog, excuse my French, right? A runty street mutt with an uncut tail and droopy ears. Have you seen dogs whose ears and tail haven't been cut? Ugh, awful. Worse than that.

Well, you can imagine, right? The mutt starts to bark, Buba starts to bark, tempers heat up, the Revlon conditioners are on sale only if you buy a shampoo, Niki is still taking a dump, and suddenly Buba is going after the other dog, barking, biting. What always happens, except for the truck. The truck, there was no way to predict it because, I mean, I can't tell the future. You know what I mean, right? I heard the squeal of the brakes and the whining of the dog. To tell you the truth, it was such a faggoty little whine I thought the mutt had been run over.

But that isn't what happened.

When Niki came out of the bathroom and saw his dog, I was already looking for places to hide. Niki kneeled beside Buba, kissed his wounds, stood, came directly toward me. I greeted him with a smile, thinking look, how great, right? We're alive, I mean, it could've been worse. And he greeted me with four shots from the Umarex CPSport. The Umarex CPSport is yellow. Have you ever seen a yellow pistol? Niki has one.

The rest of being dead is routine. You know what I mean, right? It's boring, because now nobody who's alive listens to you. It's true, they come for you, they carry you on a stretcher,

I mean, you're already dead but they still carry you on a stretcher and put you in an ambulance. Pretty weird, right? Like you were alive. That makes you feel good, right? Pretty rich. They take you to a private clinic, fill out some papers, and keep you there. It's cold there.

Very cold.

You meet other corpses, you compare yourself to them, you realize you look much better than they do, I mean, you look good in spite of the difficulties, right? And that's important to feel good about yourself. Sure, the wound doesn't help, but you can't imagine how the people there are. Huh? I mean, they don't take care of themselves. And they're respectable people. Huh? Don't think they take just any corpse to one of those clinics.

Especially at first you feel pretty insecure. It's like you got your period but it never stopped and came through your chest. Then, it's pretty uncomfortable. But then a really handsome doctor comes in. You know what I mean, right? Then you and he are alone, but not like with Buba in the car, it's different, because you're dead and he's not a dog, it's more intimate, you know? And he begins to touch you, caress you, massage you, he passes his hands along your body. And his hands are warm. Most living things are warm. And then he slits you open to find things inside you. And you know what? You feel...I don't know...you feel it's the first time a man's had any interest in your insides. I don't know. It's, like, very personal. But you let him, you let his hands go over your anatomy, you think nobody had ever touched you seriously before. And it makes you a little sad, really. There are things

I didn't know I had, that I never knew about in my life, like the duodenum, the aorta, the sternocleidomastoid, right? The triceps I did know about, from the gym. And you say to yourself damn, I would've liked to know I had all this because, I don't know, right? It's part of you and you have to live with that and this man is showing it all to you. I don't know how to explain it. It's something super super personal. If I'd had fluids, I think I even would've had an orgasm. And do you know why the medical examiner does that? Why he did it to me with that affection? I don't know, I've been thinking about it a lot, you can bet, and…I think it's because with me you can't tell. Sure, if you look at me carefully you can. But at first glance you can't tell I'm dead. I think the medical examiner likes dead girls who aren't showy. I'm very simple. You too, really. If I hadn't seen your accident in the taxi, I'd even think you were alive. A person has to look very carefully to realize it, but in the end, an experienced eye can tell.

It's your eyes, I think.

You have a dead man's eyes.